COGNITION CHRONICLES: DESTINY'S ORPHANS

J.R. BALE

ISBN-13: 978-0-9967610-3-1

This is a work of fiction. Any resemblance of characters to real people is purely coincidental.

Books by J.R. Bale

> ***Phoenix in the Middle of the Road***
> ***Cognition Chronicles: The Redstone Legacy***
> ***Cognition Chronicles: Destiny's Orphans***

Learn more about the author at www.jrbale.com.

Cover design by Balefire Communications LLC

Published by CopperKnight.

ACKNOWLEDGMENTS

Special thanks to the Watchung Writers and the Novelists Group for their valuable feedback and encouragement. Also special thanks to Elissa Matthews, Francis Ziegler and Vivian Fransen. No dedication would be complete without mentioning the support of my wife.

CHAPTER 1

"…Four-Three-Two-One. *Twist!*" the pilot of the *Sarania* called out.

Each member of the crew reacted differently to the twist, but the discomfort was universal. Despite the enormous distance covered in a matter of minutes, no one ever looked forward to a twist, only to it being over. This extreme discomfort was the price they paid for warping and twisting the fabric of the universe to obtain faster-than-light travel. At the very least, everyone felt sick to their stomachs, a sensation that often persisted for several minutes after the twist was complete. Some compared it to an instant hangover. One member of the crew described it as having one's organs pulled out and stuffed back in at the same time. Understandably, most of the crew fasted before undergoing the twist. It was a purely neurological reaction, one with no lasting side effects. At least that's what the neurologists said, the ones safely on their home planet of Refugia.

This is what you get when you try to bully space-time, thought Jason Ford, the mission's only historian. Jason waited, gripping the armrests with white knuckles, and desperately hoped to avoid vomiting.

He watched their commander Garris Enberg to see how he was reacting. He had to give the old man credit; he never threw up during a twist, not once—although Jason wouldn't have minded seeing that, putting a crack in his perfect armor. That was a pettiness Jason would never speak out loud. Enberg was too well respected for open ridicule.

Jason felt the acidy taste at the back of his throat, but suppressed the urge successfully. *Practice makes perfect.* He focused on breathing through his nose. That had helped him get through the previous 18 twists. Yet, the minutes still seemed like hours. Maybe they were, considering what they were doing to space-time.

"And we are clear," pilot Kai Herstonick finally announced.

Everyone on the flight deck gave a communal sigh of relief.

"Status of the drive system?" Commander Enberg asked.

"Torus emitters 1 through 4 are stabilized," Kai reported, knowing the enormous toruses, which encircled the *Sarania*, were the key element that twisted space-time to their will.

"Good job, Kai," said Enberg, who then keyed the intercom mic on his collar to speak to the entire crew. "Attention, we've now returned to normal space." Most members of the crew would have sensed this anyway, but Jason noticed such an announcement helped the crew recover quicker, himself included.

Enberg ran his fingers through his short graying hair, taking a deep breath. He then slapped their navigator Andy Barosi on the shoulder.

"Okay Andy, you're up. Find out exactly where the heck we came out. Should be getting close. Give me your report as soon as possible."

"Aye, sir," said Andy.

Despite being the youngest on board, Andy Barosi had the most formal demeanor. Jason thought after 19 twists and so many light years, Andy would have loosened up a bit. *Ah, the insecurity of youth.*

Enberg unstrapped himself and floated toward the rear hatch. After a twist he never hovered over Andy and Kai while they calculated the ship's new position. Jason knew exactly where Enberg was headed: Engineering. The commander could have asked for a report over the intercom, but he always liked to check on the drive systems himself. But he also had another reason.

Enberg maneuvered his way through the hatch at the rear of the flight deck and floated into the central core passageway, which extended throughout the complete length of the ship. Jason watched as Enberg pulled in his legs, positioned his feet against the bulkhead and propelled himself back along the entire central core toward the drive section in a single push. Despite the central core being almost 80 meters long, his aim was perfect. Everyone knew how Enberg enjoyed zero-G. It was his one vice, if you could call it that. The way he would propel himself down the core after a twist reminded Jason of the flying superman, an ancient Earth legend. *Perhaps the original superman was also a spacecraft commander.*

Jason unstrapped himself, too. He couldn't help Kai and Andy anyway. Although he monitored the twist readings, he was on the flight deck more as a courtesy. Technically, Jason was third in command, but it was almost an honorary position, more like a consolation prize for not receiving command of the mission himself. To qualify for this mission, Jason had learned astronomy, ship operations and orbital mechanics. He also spent thousands of hours qualifying as a lander pilot. Jason even endeavored to learn the theoretical aspects of the twist drive. Despite all this, he had been passed over for command of the mission. Instead, command was given to Garris Enberg. "A fireweeder of all people," Jason once commented snobbishly. While Jason initially resented Enberg's appointment, he respected the man's leadership and had come to like him personally.

Enberg and Kai Herstonick would have to disappear for him to ever actually take command of the *Sarania* or the mission. But there was no place for them to go. There were no ports-of-call in interstellar space. No member of the crew had left the *Sarania* in four years. His only real authority would be deciding which artifacts they would bring back from Earth.

Just as Enberg reached the far end of the corridor, the rest of the crew began to emerge from their twist stations along the central core. Most would climb down to the rotating rings where the centrifugal force provided an artificial gravity. Jason was about to launch himself toward one of the spoke ladders when he saw the ship's chief medical officer, "Doc" Skonauer. Doc was about the same age as Enberg but looked older with his white thinning hair.

"How's your stomach?" Jason asked Doc, who was floating toward the flight deck.

"Same as usual," Doc said.

"That bad?" he joked.

Doc smiled, pulled out a specially formulated antacid tablet and offered it to Jason. He shook his head, declining the tablet. He could have used one, but his pride made him decline the offer.

"Any word on how far we've come this time?" Doc asked.

"Too early to tell. But Andy's working on it. But I expect he'd appreciate one of those. Kai, too," Jason said, gesturing to Skonauer's box of antacids. "She looked a little greener this time around."

Doc nodded and, using the handholds, pushed himself toward the flight deck.

○ ● ○ ● ○

Jason climbed down the spoke ladder to Ring 2. In the ship's mess, he located Reese Monsell, the mission's chief biologist, who also served as the ship's head chef. He found her scowling over a tablet. Jason guessed she was reviewing the menu for the feast she usually prepared for the crew once everyone was past their post-twist symptoms.

Jason always showed up here after a twist, long before the feast was ready. Reese's presence always gave him a sense of calm. *Much better than an antacid.*

"How are you holding up?" she asked without looking up.

"Well, I didn't get sick, if that's what you mean," Jason said. "Hopefully, there won't be many more of these damn twists."

"With luck, we'll reach Earth soon," she said. "One more twist, two at the most I hear."

"Don't forget the way back to Refugia," he groaned. "That's got to be another 20."

"I thought with all the dark matter mapping they've done," she said, "it'll make the transit time shorter and the twists fewer."

"Hopefully," Jason said. "But with the universe expanding it could just as easily be a longer trip. We won't know until we return."

"Well," she said, "in the meantime, I need to harvest some berries. Want to help?"

"Sure."

Jason followed her back into the galley. Reese picked up a couple of wire baskets and handed one to Jason. From there, they entered the fruit-bearing agro section, which was adjacent to the galley.

"I'm thinking a blueberry crisp with a queelnut topping," Reese suggested. "What do you think?"

"Sounds great. The crew loves you for that," Jason said. "And despises me," he added in a murmur.

"Enough of your post-twist moodiness, mister," Reese said in a mock-bossy voice. "Listen. You've been training this crew for the most comprehensive archeological expedition ever attempted in human history. That will be appreciated once we arrive."

There was no designated morale officer onboard. But if there were one, she would be it. Reese gestured to a row of blueberry bushes she wanted Jason to start picking from.

"Yeah," Jason said, "but on board, I feel more like a nagging schoolmaster. Half of them skip class, and few do any of the homework."

"I tell you what," Reese said. "Let's switch. You be the chef, and I'll be the history professor."

"I'd rather switch with Enberg."

"Oh please, not that again," Reese said. "You'd think after four years you'd be over that. Besides, one or two more twists to Earth and you'll be at the center of this expedition. I thought you'd be more excited."

Jason sighed, looking down at the harvesting basket as he added another handful of berries.

"I thought I'd be more excited, too. But the more I prepare, the more I realize we're headed toward the biggest graveyard in history. The cradle of humanity is also its grave. How's that for irony?"

Jason regretted sharing his melancholy with Reese, the bright spot of his journey. Living years on the same ship without anything mission-critical to do was stressful for many of the crew. Beyond the flight and engineering teams, each crew member had a mission duty and a shipboard duty. The time of the physicists and engineers was taken up with how the twist drive performed in interstellar space and how it was affected by dark matter and dark energy.

Reese was a top-drawer biologist, specializing in the effects of radiation on life forms, particularly plant life. Earth might yield abundant plants to study, unless the planet was a completely burnt-out cinder, as some hypothesized. Or it might provide plant fossils. But in the meantime, she managed the on-ship farm and served as head chef, which made her a favorite among the crew.

Jason's shipboard duty was to teach the rest of the crew about Earth before the Great Burning, preparing them for what they might encounter on Earth, to give their future discoveries some context. But the scientists and engineers on board weren't the most enthusiastic history buffs.

Of the crew of 15, only two planetary scientists came close to Jason's situation. However, they had shipboard assignments in astronomy so they were at least making some new discoveries along the way.

"Come with me back to the galley," Reese said. "Help me prepare dinner. In fact, you can make the dessert and tell the crew it comes from an ancient Earth recipe."

"Then we'll have to leave out the queelnuts. They didn't have those on Earth."

She smiled. "As if they'd know the difference."

CHAPTER 2

That evening, the crew enjoyed their traditional post-twist feast. Reese served a tomato and basil pie and potato dumplings with her freshest herbs. As usual, delicious food served as an incredible morale booster. The blueberry crisp proved to be a particular hit. The bridge crew usually arrived last after a twist, but tonight they were later than usual, which left more time for wagering on how far from optimal the twist was. Optimal referred to the target distance the ship would travel. The ship rarely achieved that distance, and thus the opportunity for some wagering.

Enberg, Kai and Andy finally climbed down the spoke ladder. The crew stood up. Commander Enberg had long told them no such custom was required, but the mock respect seemed to amuse many of the crew so they did it anyway. The long tedium of a four-year flight prompted the occasional ritual silliness. With a smirk on his face, Enberg waved them to sit.

"So how close to optimal twist was the closest wager?" Enberg asked.

"Three million kilometers below optimal," someone called out. "That was Covarti's bet."

"Hmm," Enberg said cryptically. He picked up one of Reese's leftover hors d'oeuvres from a mostly empty platter and popped it in his mouth to create a little suspense. "Congratulations, Lyla."

Dr. Lyla Covarti stood and smiled broadly. "Never doubt an engineer!"

No one ever doubted Lyla Covarti. Among a crew of top scientists and engineers, her intellect was probably the best.

Even as a child prodigy, she kept her university professors on their toes.

The others laughed as she held up her tablet to display the tabulation of her winnings. Her winnings consisted of IOUs, payable upon completion of the mission, once they returned to Refugia—although some were duty-shift IOUs for performing the more mundane chores of other crew members. Lyla had racked up an impressive collection of winning bets but seemed to be holding back on collecting them for some unknown reason. Some theorized that winning itself was what satisfied her more than the prizes. Others thought she was saving up the duty-shift IOUs for the return flight.

"Anyway," Enberg continued, "it turns out we *exceeded* optimal by seven million kilometers. And we're only 0.43 degrees off vector. Our best twist yet. While not within the heliopause, we are at the outer edges of the Oort Cloud."

"Woo hoo!" someone called out.

Others cheered with similar enthusiasm.

"What's a heliopause and this Oort Cloud thing?" Reese whispered to Jason.

"The Oort Cloud," Jason explained, "is the outermost region of frozen ices at the edge of a solar system. The heliopause is the boundary between a star's solar wind and interstellar space. Once we pass inside the heliopause, we'll be somewhat shielded from the interstellar cosmic radiation by the solar wind."

"Thanks," she said. "I think I'll stick to biology."

After the cheering quieted down, Enberg added, "And our position is not even the most exciting part."

Members of the crew looked at each other perplexed. Enberg gave a barely perceptible smile, signaling the best was yet to come.

"We have our first images."

"Let's see 'em," Lyla Covarti called out. Although a meticulous and diligent engineer, she often exhibited the unbridled curiosity of a scientist.

Enberg nodded to Andy, who hit the switch to reveal the live feed on the monitors. Everyone appeared hypnotized by the images on the screen. Except for the hum of equipment, the room was completely quiet. Everyone was trying to make sense of what they were witnessing.

"Did Sol turn into a pulsar?" Jason asked. It was an understandable question given the flashing light.

"No, that's not possible," said one of the physicists. "Besides, the periodic dimming of the star isn't regular enough. There must be a set of obstacles passing between us and the star."

"The odds of any object coming between us and the star as we just come out of a twist is—well, no pun intended—astronomical," Lyla said.

"What if it's the Earth?" someone called out. "Or rather pieces of what's left of Earth after the burning?"

Everyone suddenly looked like they had undergone another twist.

"How far is the debris, or whatever it is, from the sun?" Jason asked.

"Approximately 150 million kilometers," Andy said.

"That's roughly the distance from the Earth to the sun, isn't it?" someone asked.

"No, that would be a bit beyond Earth's orbit," Jason said, "at least according to the Ark records."

"True," Enberg said. "But at our current distance, it's hard to be sure. There's only one way to find out. After all our post-twist checks and procedures are complete, I plan to move up our final twist, once the twist drive has fully recharged. Crossing through the heliopause will be tricky, but we always knew that."

None of the crew cheered over that news.

"What?" Reese mumbled to no one in particular. "He couldn't wait to announce the next twist until the meal was done?"

○ ● ○ ● ○

Later that evening Jason was sitting alone in the ship's mess with a mug of queelnut tea. The queelnut was Refugia's most versatile crop. The only thing in the Ark records he could find close to its utility was the ancient almond. Unfortunately, almonds required too much water to thrive on Refugia. He found the faint aroma of the queelnut tea quite calming.

The only sound around him was the soft hum of the atmospheric pumps. He pulled an oval medallion out of his breast pocket. Decorative ornamentation surrounded the name engraved in the center: *Jennika*.

"Well Jen," he whispered as he held the shiny medallion in his hand. "We're getting close. We'll see if you were right. And if I was wrong." He stared at the medallion, wondering what might have been if he hadn't signed onto this mission. *Marriage? Children? Promotions at the university?* Accepting the Sarania mission put that all out of reach.

"Couldn't sleep?" a soft voice said from behind him.

He turned around to see Reese. He casually tucked the medallion back into his pocket.

"No," Jason said. "How about you?"

"Grig's not feeling well. Doc has him under observation. Apparently, twists and sinus infections don't mix."

Jason chuckled. "Twists don't mix with anything, especially anything human."

"So," Reese said, "I'm covering the night shift meal."

"Ah." Jason took another sip of his tea.

"So, sitting here all alone, what's on your mind?" Reese asked.

"Do you really want to know?" he asked. "You had to listen to my moodiness earlier. Sorry about that."

"I've got a few minutes. What's percolating in that brain of yours?"

"Debris," he said.

"By debris, you mean Earth debris?"

"*Possible* Earth debris." Jason nodded and leaned back in his chair. "Did you know there was strong opposition to my being assigned to this mission?"

Reese turned her head oddly at the sudden change of topic.

"Well," she said, "the selection process was very competitive."

"That's not what I mean," Jason said. "If you weren't selected, they would've choosen another biologist in your place."

"Not as good though," she joked.

"True," he said, smiling. "And if Lyla Covarti weren't selected, another engineer would be serving in her place. In fact, all of you have backups. You have Grig. Lyla has Glates. Even Enberg has Kai Herstonick. But I have no backup. Ever notice that?"

"I assumed we were all your backup. That's what all the history classes were about, weren't they?"

Jason shook his head no.

"Director Quertsa was vehemently opposed to having a historian, any historian, on the mission. He felt the crew should just record what they find and bring it back."

"Really?" Reese said, "I never knew that. As the Director General of the Refugian Space Administration, I thought Quertsa's word was law. How did you overcome his objections?"

"I don't know that I ever did," he answered. "But the university held the original Ark records. And they leveraged that to get a seat for a historian on board. To go on this mission, I gave up my position as a professor and curator of the Earth Museum. I learned how to fly and obtained other technical certifications."

"Why go to all that trouble," Reese asked, "if you weren't wanted?"

"Everything we know about Earth is from the Ark records. No other sources. I know I would shock some of my colleagues, but how do we know they're accurate? Or even complete? And some of the Ark records do have inconsistencies. So, I want proof. I want to round out our knowledge of humanity's home, answering that existential question: Who are we really?" Jason took another sip of his tea. "And now after jumping all those hurdles and enduring all those damn twists, we find bloody debris! It may have all been for nothing."

"Well, the same may be said for all of us."

"No, not exactly." Jason shook his head. "Even if we don't find Earth intact, Covarti and her engineers will have operational data on the first long-distance twist drive. The physicists will have gathered an unprecedented amount of data on dark matter and other interstellar phenomena. You will have maintained the largest and most sustained astro-farm ever."

"Well, my dear historian," Reese said in a deliberately condescending tone, "don't think you're the only one who will get screwed. If we don't find an intact planet, people will only remember me as the chef of the *Sarania*. *The cook.* But, as you know, I'm a full-blown environmental biologist. I gave up a lot too. Did you know I was being considered for a senior director position at the Environmental Ministry?"

"No, I didn't." Jason raised his mug toward Reese. "Madame Director."

"Okay, Mr. Historian, you have scoured the Ark records for clues to human history. And, as you've just indicated, you want to verify it. But what about before humans existed? What do you know about extinction events?"

"Like the Great Burning?"

"Yeah, yeah, every child who studies Earth history or the Ark knows about the Great Burning over 2000 years ago. But did you know there were several extinction events on Earth before that?"

"Vaguely," Jason murmured.

"About 65 million years ago an asteroid struck Earth, wiping out many species, including the most dominant group at the time, the dinosaurs. Over 186 million years before that, a large volcano erupted, wiping out 96 percent of all life on Earth. *Ninety-six percent!* That one, the Permian–Triassic extinction event, was called the Great Dying. Think how far evolution was set back. And there were several other extinction events before that."

"And your point is?" Jason asked.

"After each of these events, life came back," she continued. "Not the same life but life of some sort. I want to understand how. Could there be some new form of life that has evolved on Earth, something completely alien? Something weird? Something glorious?"

"But if the Earth is just orbital debris—"

"Then there's nothing for either of us to study," she said. "What was the point of us learning how to be lander pilots if there's nothing to land on?" She placed her hand on his. "In the end, we may have nothing but each other."

Chapter 3

As the thousands of delegates were milling around to find their places, President Pegg Maklund tapped her gavel to begin the meeting of the Spherical Council. Its unique resonating crack was one of her guilty pleasures. Rather than metal, plastic or some other synthetic material, it was made of a rare material: wood. While she valued its history as an ancient gavel passed down through her family, its sound was what she loved most. With the combination of the gavel and the unusual acoustics of the enormous council chamber, no one else could make that exact sound.

Nysandra Trin, the President's First Minister, approached.

"Madame President," Trin said. "Director Graith says he needs to see you immediately."

"Now? That man has such a sense of self-importance," she muttered under her breath.

"Madame President!" an impatient voice called out.

Maklund recognized the voice of Symas Graith, head of the astro-mining directorate, as he came rushing up to her. She found him quite wearing when he was after something.

"Director Graith, don't worry, she said. "Your infrastructure proposal is on the agenda as promised. Let me finish calling the Council to order."

"I'm not here about infrastructure," Graith answered. "An emergency has come up."

"Let me guess," Maklund said. "A rogue asteroid?"

"No."

"Then how can your directorate have an emergency that requires the immediate attention of the Spherical Council?"

Maklund asked, trying to hide her impatience. "Can't it wait a few minutes?"

"Not the Council's attention. Yours." Graith walked around to the side of her desk and leaned in. "I think we're being invaded," he whispered urgently.

"Invaded?" Maklund wondered what kind of political maneuvering this was. "By whom?"

"Aliens," he said, "for lack of a better term."

"Graith, I don't have time for such nonsense!"

"It is *not* nonsense," Graith said. "And you had better make time."

Maklund often found Graith irritating, but he was never this brazen. She turned back to the Council and banged the gavel, this time with no pleasure.

"My apologies, everyone. We will have a short delay before coming to order. Use the time to find your seats, please."

The audience gave a communal groan as she left the dais. Maklund escorted Graith into her private office, off the main chamber. She found other senior officials from the directorate waiting for her, all of them scowling or frowning.

"Very well, Symas," Maklund said. "What is this about?"

"We've discovered an object just within the heliopause. It wasn't there and then it was."

"A scanning malfunction or negligent technician. So what?" Maklund sat down behind her desk. "Congratulations, you have another asteroid to mine."

"It's not an asteroid, Madame President. It's a ship or a probe, or something like that. It appeared, then shortly after that *changed course*. Asteroids don't change course, at least not without our help."

"The SolarSphere has thousands of ships," Maklund said, trying not to roll her eyes. "Did somebody lose one? Perhaps we have another rogue ship or a smuggler?"

"No, and it's not one of ours." He pressed a button to display the ship on a monitor. It was long with four ring-shaped projections around it. "It's massive for a ship, over 100 meters long. Even our largest asteroid catchers are barely that large. And a smuggler wouldn't use a ship that size. Too conspicuous. Besides, what would they be smuggling out at the edge of the solar system? Here is a more detailed report." He handed the President the file on a tablet.

As Maklund read the report, Nysandra Trin walked up to Graith.

"Does this," she whispered, "have anything to do with *them*?"

"I can't imagine," Graith said, closing his eyes. "I certainly hope not."

Maklund looked up from the report. "Have you tried communicating with it?"

"No," Graith answered. "As this is what I am told is called a *First Contact*, we thought you as president should be notified before any action is taken."

Maklund sighed. "Ask them to identify themselves."

"We should consider carefully what our first message should be," Trin said. "The ramifications might be considerable. What if they are hostile? On the other hand, what if they are friendly?"

"Either way, asking them to identify themselves is probably a good start."

○ ● ○ ● ○

Jason floated among the others on the flight deck, grinning at the monitor. It wasn't debris. *It wasn't debris!* he thought with glee.

"I'll be a son of a fireweeder," Jason muttered absentmindedly as he looked at the screen.

Everyone on the flight deck stared at him, looking awkward. Jason started to perspire immediately. His joy was suddenly replaced by embarrassment.

"I'm sorry, Commander," he said. "That was insensitive and inappropriate. It won't happen again."

"Forget it," Enberg said, gesturing to the screen. "Let's focus on the task at hand."

They had completed another twist, a mere three weeks after the previous one, a ship record. Now they were viewing an enhanced image of the star.

"As we can see," said Lyla Covarti, "whatever is passing between us and Earth's sun seems to be a series of connected structures. It's huge. Actually, huge doesn't even cover it. If this structure completely surrounds the sun, it will have a circumference of over a billion kilometers."

"Like a ring?" Enberg asked.

"Whew, that's one hell of a ring," Kai said.

"It's a fairly wide ring, too," said Andy, who was monitoring the video feed. "It extends almost a million kilometers above and below the orbital plane. It also curves inward, so each part seems to be equidistant from the sun."

"I think I know what we're looking at," Covarti said. "It makes perfect sense."

"A Dyson Sphere?" Jason guessed.

"Exactly," Lyla said. "Or at least one in the making."

"Excuse me, what's a Dyson Sphere?" Andy asked.

"It's a theoretical structure—well, perhaps not so theoretical, given what we're seeing," Covarti said, looking at the monitor. "Anyway, the idea is that it completely surrounds a star, capturing as much of its energy output as possible. I'm willing to bet the other side of that thing—the inside—is lined with solar panels."

"Wait, something's happening," Andy said. "Commander, there are three contacts—I assume ships—approaching us."

"Are they in formation?"

"Formation?"

"I mean are they traveling in close proximity or on the same course?"

"No, sir," Andy said. "They seem to be coming from different directions. I calculate the nearest one will take nine hours to reach us."

"It seems we've been noticed," Enberg said. "I guess we should formally announce ourselves."

Enberg turned to Lyla. "Can we transmit on multiple frequencies simultaneously?"

"That will take some doing," Lyla said. "We weren't expecting—"

"That's okay. Start with the old Ark frequencies and record this message."

Lyla nodded, indicating she was ready. Enberg pressed the mic button on his collar.

"This is Commander Garris Enberg of the interstellar spacecraft *Sarania* from the Earth colony Refugia."

To Jason, it felt odd to hear their home planet described as an Earth colony. But that was exactly what Refugia started out as.

Enberg looked at Jason and the others, appearing a little embarrassed at the cliché he was about to deliver.

"We come in peace," Enberg continued. "Please respond." He clicked off his mic and turned back to Lyla. "Try sending and repeating that message on as many frequencies as possible."

Everyone waited anxiously, but there was no response.

"Any ideas?" Enberg looked around. "Anyone?"

"We assume they speak our language," Jason said. "But Earth had many languages."

"Do you know any of these languages?" Enberg asked.

"No, we weren't expecting anyone alive. All I have are programs for translating texts." Jason looked around the flight deck. "Also, we have translation programs for written materials we might find on Earth, but that's it." Then, looking around an idea occurred to Jason. "We could try transmitting pulses in groups of prime numbers: 1, 2, 3, 5, 7, 11, 13, 17, 19, 23."

"I know what prime numbers are," Enberg said. "But why?"

"It lets them know we're trying to communicate. Regardless of any language barrier, any reasonably advanced civilization would have an understanding of mathematics. Prime numbers would be basic enough, regardless of what mathematical system they use. Even if they weren't human."

"Okay," Enberg said, turning to Lyla. "Transmit it on all frequencies, alternating with my recorded message."

"We could even blink the external ship lights that way," Kai suggested. "If they're watching us, they'll see it."

"Good. Start blinking the lights."

Twenty minutes passed. Jason rubbed his hands together nervously. He had prepared for an archeological expedition. Now they were facing the prospect of living humans who might react in unpredictable ways.

"We're receiving a transmission," Lyla called out.

Everyone listened to the speaker carefully.

"This is Pegg Maklund, President of the Spherical Council. Please identify yourself."

"It sounds like they didn't hear your message," Kai said.

"But they speak our language," Enberg said, sounding relieved.

"Strange accent though," Lyla said.

"I'm sure our accent will sound just as strange to them," Jason said.

"Put me on the same frequency," Enberg ordered.

He repeated his initial message, emphasizing the "we come in peace" part.

"Commander Enberg? What is your intention, I mean, the purpose of your…arrival?"

"Exploration, Madame President. We are here to explore the home system of humanity."

"What species are you?"

Everyone on the flight deck chuckled. Enberg smiled.

"We are quite human. We are descendants of Earth, presumably as you are."

"Yes, quite human. Commander Enberg, welcome to the SolarSphere."

"Thank you. I have to admit we never expected to meet any humans on this mission. We believed everyone on Earth had died."

"Oh, they did."

CHAPTER 4

The *Sarania* took several more days to reach the SolarSphere. During that time, most of the communication with the Spherians, as the crew had come to call them, were navigational directions relayed by an escort vessel. Its commander, Captain Torg, was reluctant to answer too many non-navigational questions, although she did reveal her ship was an "asteroid catcher." Lyla Covarti was particularly interested in the design, studying the enormous red manipulator arms and imagining the ship in operation. There were markings on the ship, AC1065, which suggested this craft was probably part of a fleet of over a thousand.

Jason was pleased they used the numerals and letters. This would make learning from their records easier.

They were within a few thousand miles of the sphere, which now completely filled all viewports facing the structure like a giant wall. The *Sarania* was now traveling parallel to the surface of the sphere, although the term surface was not completely accurate. The exterior of the structure was more like a cage with large rotating cylinders in the gaps.

Lyla had her camera out recording like a tourist, but her demeanor was quite intense.

"That's it!" she cried out in excitement.

"What it?" Reese asked, who was floating nearby.

"Those cylinders are rotating once every seven to eight minutes, and they're about 250 kilometers in diameter! Don't you see what they are?"

"No," said Reese. "What are they?"

"Habitats, delivering the equivalent of one G of artificial gravity, just like our rings. And if the entire ring or sphere is made of these habitats, it could be holding trillions of human beings. This is the opposite of what we expected!"

"Not necessarily," Reese said. "There's something you've forgotten."

"What?"

"The resources required to support such a population. If they are habitats, they'll need a way to produce food, either agriculturally or industrially."

"Hmm…Well, I guess we have a lot of questions to ask these people." Lyla grinned broadly. "Hopefully, we'll find out soon."

○ ● ○ ● ○

Captain Torg guided the *Sarania* to an area designated as Drydock 168, which apparently specialized in maintaining and repairing their enormous asteroid catchers. Unlike the rotating cylinders, Drydock 168 was a cavernous structure, with no rotating sections to create artificial gravity.

"Captain Torg says we are to maneuver the *Sarania* inside," Kai reported. "Then the doors will close. Once closed, they'll pump in a breathable atmosphere. Then we can float to the hatch and meet our reception committee."

"We'll be trapped," Barosi said.

"Why do they want to do this?" Enberg asked.

"She says it's the only way," Kai said, "we can meet face to face. They don't have any compatible hatches for docking."

"We could send in a lander," Barosi suggested.

Enberg considered this for a moment. Then he said, "No, we need to save the landers and their fuel for Earth."

"Tell them we require the bay doors stay open...for safety purposes. We have pressure suits. We can float our way to their airlock."

Herstonick transmitted the message. After a 10-minute delay, Torg confirmed that was acceptable.

○ ● ○ ● ○

Jason was looking out of one of the viewports when Enberg approached him.

"A word?" Enberg tilted his head toward his quarters.

Jason followed.

Once inside, Enberg closed the door and sat. "I never expected to find any human beings on this mission, certainly not like this."

"No one did," Jason said. "We'd been led to believe all human life was wiped out in this solar system. Of course, Ark records wouldn't include what happened after the Ark left Earth."

"Regardless," Enberg said, "we've been invited to visit the Spherians at 20:00 hours. I have to admit I have no training as a diplomat. There wasn't much use for it on the Outer Scorch."

"You seemed to do just fine in your initial exchange with President Maklund."

"That was just saying hello. What do you think we can expect?"

"From these Spherians? I can't imagine. I'm a historian. My most current knowledge is well over a thousand years old."

"That's better than I have."

It wouldn't be if you showed up to my classes, Jason almost said.

"There's no way to tell how their society has evolved."

"But you understand how societies evolve or might evolve," Enberg said. "I want you to lead the—I'm not sure what to call it—landing party? Boarding party?"

"Perhaps *diplomatic delegation*? Although as I think of it, we have no authorization to represent the Refugian government."

"See, you know this stuff. You know, Quertsa didn't want you on this mission."

"Yes, I'm painfully aware of that."

"But he was wrong, dead wrong," Enberg said. "I want you to lead the party, diplomatic or otherwise."

"Really? Thank you," Jason said, smiling. Then his smile faded. "As much as I'd like to lead the party, it should be led by the mission commander. You've already spoken to President Maklund. To send to an intermediary might be considered insulting by the Spherians. We don't know what their norms of etiquette might be. I'd hate to insult them."

Enberg nodded.

"You're right, I suppose," he said. "Okay, be ready to suit up at the aft airlock at 18:30. I still want you with me."

"Will it be just you and me?" Jason asked.

"I'll have Lyla Covarti join us. I'd like to get her assessment of their technology. Doesn't hurt to have another set of eyes. See you at 18:30 hours."

Jason nodded and started to leave.

"You know, as a historian I just expected to discover and record history. But now   we're about to make history."

Enberg smiled. "Isn't that awful?"

○ ● ○ ● ○

Once Enberg announced the party, many of the crew tried to make a case for themselves to be included, but Enberg held firm. He said he wanted to keep the initial party small.

Covarti and Enberg had no problem putting on their pressure suits, but Jason took longer. Although he had trained for it, Jason never expected to actually have to don such equipment on this mission.

Enberg opened the hatch and swung himself through the airlock with the grace of a gymnast. Jason was impressed, considering Enberg's large build. Jason was second to move out with Lyla picking up the rear.

Jason had spacewalked before as part of their training in orbit above Refugia. However, entering this cavernous structure was slightly disorienting.

Once all three were outside the ship, Enberg attached a long line to his suit. The other end was linked to an external handhold. Enberg held onto the metal loop with his left hand. He placed one foot on either side, bending his knees as far as the bulky pressure suit would allow. Releasing the handhold, his legs extended, launching himself across the enormous space toward a platform inside the bay. All his post-twist pushes down the central core had served him well.

However, Enberg started to tumble. This was much farther than the central core of the *Sarania*, which the Commander was used to.

So much for Enberg's grace, Jason thought.

Enberg banged awkwardly against the platform sideways and started to bounce away. Luckily, he was able to catch a railing with his foot. This changed his trajectory, enabling him to grab a handhold on the wall. From there, he maneuvered himself back to the platform. Enberg then took the line attached to his suit and tied it to the handhold. Now Jason and Lyla could pull themselves across the bay much more easily than Enberg.

Jason grabbed the line to pull himself over. It was not as taut as he expected. He pulled himself forward, which gave him momentum, but then he was jerked back by his grasp on the line, which knocked the wind out of him. He tried to pull himself hand over hand. The momentum increased.

"Slow down," Enberg said over the commlink. "Otherwise, you'll hit the wall harder than I did."

Jason applied a little friction to the line in his glove. It was working. He finally reached Enberg.

"Good job," Enberg said. "Now you see one reason I wanted to keep the party small."

He turned back toward the *Sarania*. "Okay, Lyla. Your turn."

"Great, I can't wait."

She took a different approach, launching herself off the side of the *Sarania* in the same way Enberg did. She didn't grasp the line but rather positioned it in the crook of her arm. Eventually, she grabbed the line with her glove and slowed using slight fiction.

Lyla wins the most elegant crossing award, Jason thought.

As they all pulled themselves into the platform area, Jason noticed many windows with several faces peering out at them. "We have an audience."

"And they look human," Enberg said. "That's a good sign."

At that moment a large octagonal airlock door slowly swung open.

"I think," Lyla said, "that's our cue."

The three of them floated into the spacious airlock. There were controls inside the airlock, but someone else seemed to be handling the pressurization remotely. Eventually, their suit indicators read close to normal but not quite.

"Atmospheric readings indicate a nitrogen-oxygen atmosphere similar to ours," Lyla reported. "But the pressure in here is slightly higher."

"Good. Adjust your suit pressures to match the environment," Enberg ordered, which required less than a minute. "I'll go first," he said.

Covarti positioned herself close to Enberg, in case anything went wrong. He opened the visor of his helmet just a few centimeters.

"Don't forget to swallow," Lyla said. "The pressure won't be exact."

"I'm good. The air smells okay."

After a minute, they all removed their helmets. At that moment, the other hatch opened. At the other end of that chamber was a man, holding an instrument to his face and pointing it at them, without making any attempt to move.

Is he pointing a weapon at us? Jason thought

Suddenly, a woman and another man came floating from behind him.

"Greetings," the woman said. "I am First Minister Nysandra Trin. On behalf of President Maklund and all the biospheres of the SolarSphere, I welcome you."

They regarded the woman briefly but focused on the man behind her, who was still pointing his equipment at them. She turned to see what they were looking at.

"Oh, that's Glynn. He's recording this momentous event for posterity. I hope we have not offended you."

"No offense taken," Enberg said. "We just didn't understand. I am Commander Garris Enberg of the *Sarania*. This is Dr. Lyla Covarti and Dr. Jason Ford. We're very pleased to meet you." He looked around. "I was expecting your President Maklund."

"As her First Minister, I'm here to greet and escort you to her," Trin said. "I admit I'm at a disadvantage. We have no protocols for meeting beings from another solar system."

"Neither do we," Enberg said. "We can develop our protocols together."

"Um, perhaps you would like to remove your environmental suits and be more comfortable. You can store them in this storage compartment. We will place a guard on them. No one will touch your equipment, I promise."

"Some trust is appropriate," Jason whispered to Enberg.

"Yes," Enberg said, "but all we have underneath are our cooling garments. We'd be making First Contact in the equivalent of our underwear."

"That'll be a story to tell." Lyla chuckled in a low voice. "Besides, who knows what their underwear looks like? They might not notice."

After removing their pressure suits and stowing them in a storage compartment, they came out. The concerned expression on Trin's face was obvious.

"I apologize for the appearance of our cooling garments."

"They are rather conspicuous," Trin said. "To be honest, we have not revealed your arrival to the general population yet."

She then turned to her aide. "Can we find them something to wear?"

Trin quickly turned back. "If that is acceptable."

"That's fine," Enberg said. "Thank you."

Trin's aide nodded and left. Within a few minutes, he returned with what looked like light gray coveralls. Once the *Sarania* crew put them on, they followed Trin and Glynn through another octagonal hatch, then down a corridor and into a room where all the seats were facing the same direction. Trin's aide stayed behind.

"This is a sliptube capsule, our primary mode of transportation within the Sphere. The sliptube network can take us anywhere in Sphere. Please be seated, at least during the initial acceleration."

"Acceleration?" Jason asked, looking at the chairs, which looked more like contoured couches with head supports.

"Yes, of course," Covarti said. "The odds of us arriving at a convenient point on such a large structure were incredibly remote. How far will we need to travel?"

"Not far," Trin said. "Just a half million kilometers."

"A half million?" Jason repeated.

"Given the sphere has a circumference of nearly a billion kilometers," Lyla said, "that's a short hop."

"That's why we directed you to Drydock 168," Trin said. "It is the closest such facility to GovCenter."

Trin sat in the front seat. She gestured for Enberg to sit next to her. A flat control panel was mounted between the two seats. Covarti and Ford sat in the following row, while Glynn and one of the two escorts sat further back.

They watched Trin place a small cylinder into the corner of the control panel, then punch in some settings on the screen.

"Is everyone seated properly?" Trin looked back at Jason and Lyla and seemed satisfied. "Initializing transit." She pressed a wide bar at the bottom of the control screen.

Acceleration pushed them back in their seats. However, Jason noticed it didn't have the shaking of aerial resistance one experienced on a lift-off from a planet's surface. He looked at Lyla next to him, whom he suspected was thinking the same thing.

"Excuse me, Minister Trin," Lyla began. "Is there a vacuum in these sliptubes?"

"Yes, there is. I'm not a technician, but I believe it's necessary to achieve the speeds we require."

"And how fast are we traveling?"

"I'm not exactly sure. Our speed will be constantly changing."

"Currently, we're still accelerating. How long will our trip take?"

"Approximately 45 minutes."

"That's roughly 600,000 kilometers per hour," Lyla concluded out loud. "That means we'll experience some time dilation."

"A little bit," Trin said.

She says this as if it were nothing, Jason thought to himself. *Apparently to her, it's business as usual.*

Jason looked over at Lyla grinning.

Eventually, the acceleration ceased. Zero-gravity began. Then the seats rotated 180 degrees, followed by deceleration.

Finally, the sliptube capsule slowed to a stop. Once they unstrapped themselves and floated out of the capsule, they were guided to an elevator.

"Be sure to hold onto the handles," Trin warned.

As they descended, artificial gravity began to exert its influence. Standing and walking replaced floating.

"We must be descending into one of those rotating cylinders," Lyla Coverti whispered.

As they stepped out of the elevator, Jason felt slightly disoriented. The chamber was dark. It took a moment for Jason's eyes to adjust. The space was enormous, kilometers across. Looking up was like viewing a nighttime aerial photograph of a town or city at night. The subdued lighting revealed the ceiling was a geometric arrangement of buildings and parks. The city on the "ceiling" extended down along curved walls. *A cylindrical city held in place by centrifugal force.*

Jason could see Enberg looking up as well, just as mesmerized. Lyla, on the other hand, was grinning. She looked over at Jason and mouthed, *I was right.*

"GovCenter is in night mode right now," Trin explained.

"They do this to maintain a circadian rhythm," he murmured, which was advisable for a species that evolved on a planet. *After all, they are also descendants of Earth.*

"Right this way," Trin said, guiding them to the largest nearby building, which had a large spherical dome at the top. Once inside, they were led into a chamber where a tall woman with gray hair greeted them.

"Commander Enberg," Trin said, "I present Pegg Maklund, President of the SolarSphere."

"It is a pleasure to meet you, Madame President," Enberg said.

"It is an honor to meet you, Commander Enberg."

Enberg then introduced Jason and Lyla. "We have so many questions."

"As do we," Maklund said. "For instance, if you're not from the SolarSphere, where exactly did you come from?"

"A planet called Refugia," Enberg answered. "It was colonized by humans from Earth roughly 2000 years ago. Our ancestors on the Ark believed everyone left behind on Earth would soon be extinct. Obviously, they were wrong."

"No, they were quite correct. All humanity on Earth died out almost as long ago, long before the Sphere was built."

"Forgive me. How is that possible?" Jason asked. "I mean you're standing here, very much alive."

Maklund smiled. "Please sit down. It seems strange to have to explain a story we all grew up with, one we tell our children. After the Great Burning robots resurrected humanity from frozen embryos."

"Frozen embryos?" Jason interjected. "So there *was* a plan for survival."

"No, I don't think so," Maklund said, shaking her head. "Our historians seem to agree; it was an unplanned and unlikely series of events. Embryos were frozen from an earlier time for people who had fertility problems. Then after the Great Burning, robots nurtured these embryos. Many of the details are unclear. But whatever the truth is, those embryos were destiny's orphans, left behind by sheer chance."

"The robots," Jason said, "must have been programmed to do this."

"Our historians say no. The robots were programmed to tend to the needs of humans. Once there were no humans, I suppose they went on to the next best thing."

"I just don't see how that's possible," Lyla said. "A robot's programming isn't that intuitive."

"I'll admit it is an incredible story. Software specialists who have studied the matter say it was probably a fluke result of their programming, but there's no way to be certain. Perhaps there are errors in our history. But it was what we were taught growing up. But our historians have not been able to refute it."

"Those would have been very advanced AI robots," said Lyla. "I'd love to see one."

"While we have industrial robots, I'm afraid that type is long gone. We were never able to reproduce such technology. Those orphans lived in domes created by their ancestors on Earth's surface, as the outside environment was too inhospitable. The planet's environment became increasingly unstable. So those humans migrated to space stations and then built more in solar orbit. Eventually, those space stations were connected. Then the design was extended into a ring, and now that ring is being extended into a sphere."

"It is a remarkable feat of engineering," Lyla said.

"For our ancestors, it was a feat of survival. When Earth became uninhabitable, it became a necessity." Maklund then turned to Enberg. "Commander, I would like to invite you and your crew to a formal dinner to honor your journey, your extraordinary accomplishment."

"Our accomplishment?"

"Yes, crossing interplanetary space."

"Our accomplishment seems insignificant compared to yours," Enberg said, "but I humbly accept."

A mutual admiration society is forming, Jason thought to himself.

After some more small talk, Enberg, Jason and Lyla were escorted back to the airlock they had entered.

"Commander," Lyla said, "our suits have been examined or at least moved."

"How can you tell?"

"I put my gloves inside my helmet. They are not there now."

"Could they have floated away?"

"No, because they're now stowed inside my suit."

Enberg turned to Jason. "What about yours?"

Jason looked down at his pressure suit. "I can't tell."

"Have they tampered with anything?" Enberg asked, looking back to Lyla.

"I can't be sure."

"Let's make sure," Enberg said.

"What about our escorts?" Jason asked, tilting his head toward the door.

"I suspect they don't have EVA experience. Let's double-check everything."

After about 20 minutes all systems seemed to check out. They suited up and came out.

"Sorry for the delay," Jason blurted out. "Standard protocol."

Trin nodded. "Of course. I look forward to seeing you at the dinner."

The three exited the airlock to find their line where they left it.

After returning to the *Sarania*, Enberg and the others briefed the rest of the crew.

○ ● ○ ● ○

Brother Yurasti leaned over his workstation, completing his most recent analysis early. He decided to squeeze in a little physical therapy. He took off his robe, then turned and stretched the muscles of his deformed body. His physicians had suggested corrective surgery on his spine, but he refused. This was the way his kind was born. Yurasti left surgical alterations to those he monitored. However, he did perform therapeutic exercises. He stretched persistently, painful as it was. Pain was human. *Remove the pain, remove the humanity.*

Some had encouraged him to move to a low-G retirement facility. He had always refused such a suggestion. He had a sacred mission.

The door beeped.

"Master, it is Maynberc," a voice said through the door.

Yurasti quickly pulled on his robe. While his deformities were not a secret, a small speck of vanity still remained in the old man, especially when he thought of Maynberc's powerful physique.

Yurasti opened the door. The tall Maynberc entered.

"Master, there is unexpected news. We have human visitors from another world."

"Yes, I know."

Maynberc showed no expression of surprise, but that was his nature, if one could use that term.

"President Maklund hasn't announced their arrival yet," Yurasti continued. "But I expect she plans to make the news public quite soon. She is a politician after all. Their arrival is quite unexpected indeed. And possibly dangerous."

"Why dangerous?" Maynberc asked.

"They are explorers, curious by nature and vocation. They will no doubt want to explore the SolarSphere and may go places that might be inconvenient. And perhaps even interfere with our mission."

"Then it might be best to eliminate them."

Even Yurasti was taken aback by Maynberc's quick and cold logic.

"Such a drastic measure might be an overreaction," Yurasti said softly, "at least at first. It might draw attention to us and those we monitor. For now we must be vigilant."

CHAPTER 5

Enberg agreed to move the *Sarania* inside Drydock 168 and allow the outer doors to close around it. This gave the Spherians a sign of trust and made transferring to the SolarSphere much easier without pressure suits. Once the *Sarania* was secure, Enberg called the crew together in the main mess.

"President Maklund has decided to honor us," Enberg said, "with an official dinner tonight. She invited our entire crew. However, to do this would mean temporarily abandoning *Sarania*. And that I won't do."

Jason recalled the glove incident with their spacesuits. He assumed someone was simply curious. However, abandoning the *Sarania*, even temporarily, would leave the ship vulnerable to trespassing or even tampering.

"President Maklund and I," Enberg continued, "have compromised on a party of eight. I'm drafting Kai Herstonick, Lyla Covarti, Jason Ford and Doc Skonauer. There's room for three others. We can draw lots."

"Only three?" someone called out.

"Commander," Lyla Covarti said, "I'd like to volunteer to stay behind."

"Why?" Enberg said. "I assumed you would be as curious as anyone."

"Oh, I am," she said. "But we also have another opportunity. The *Sarania* is now surrounded by a breathable atmosphere. That was never supposed to happen. I'd like to take this opportunity to examine the effects of the cosmic radiation on the hull from crossing interstellar space."

"We were going to do that," Kai said, "once we were in Earth orbit."

"But now, I can do it without a pressure suit. The job will go much faster. Plus I can *feel* the effects for myself," Lyla added, rubbing her fingertips together.

"Okay," Enberg said. "Any other volunteers want to stay behind?"

No one offered.

"Okay, I guess that means there are four openings."

Once the lots were drawn, the additional members included Reese Monsell and three others.

At the appointed time, Enberg and his seven selected crewmates departed, floating out of the airlock. They wore their dress uniforms, which had been pulled out of storage. These garments were not intended to be used until their return to Refugia. Each tunic bore the *Sarania* mission insignia: a profile of a woman's face across from an illustration of Earth.

"It feels strange to exit the exterior hatch without a pressure suit on," Jason commented.

"Think that's strange?" Reese said. "Look back at the ship."

It had been four years since any of them had been outside the *Sarania*. It was truly disorienting to see the enormous *Sarania*—its four massive rings still rotating, two clockwise and two counterclockwise—completely enclosed.

Once again, Nysandra Trin, met the party and escorted them to GovCenter. And again, Glynn recorded their journey. This time the sliptube capsule was longer to accommodate the larger group.

Meanwhile, Lyla Covarti and Andy Barosi floated out of the hatch. Instead of heading toward the sphere's airlock, they pulled themselves along the exterior hull.

"Without a pressure suit, this feels soooo weird," Andy blurted out.

"Relax. The air pressure is higher out here than inside the ship. We'll be fine."

"Still. EVA without a suit?" Andy said, "It's just, well, wrong."

Covarti pulled herself along the hull of the *Sarania*. "Are you kidding? This is so much easier without a bulky suit."

She placed the sensor against the outer hull, activating the instrument.

A smile crossed her face. "Not bad." She was measuring the deterioration in the hull due to cosmic radiation. So far her readings were better than expected. She pulled herself along the hull.

"You should keep your harness tethered to the ship," warned Andy.

"Yeah, but then I couldn't fly." Lyla then pushed herself along the side of the hull about 15 meters without touching any part of the ship.

"Lyla!"

She grabbed a handhold, grinning.

"That's dangerous!" Andy warned.

"If we were in deep space or planetary orbit, I'd agree. But we're in a zero-G, enclosed, air-filled environment."

"But what if you floated away? We don't have any thruster packs on. What if you get stuck midair, unable to push against anything, unable to maneuver?"

Covarti responded by attaching her harness line to a handhold. "Watch," she said. She then puckered her lips and began blowing. She began floating away from the ship, her harness eventually becoming taut. "Built-in thruster," she said, winking. "Come on, relax and have a little fun."

○ ● ○ ● ○

The crew arrived at the reception to the sound of soft music playing. Jason noticed all heads turned toward them. During this mission he had expected to be the observer, not the observed.

President Maklund approached them, wearing a long shimmering silver and gold garment.

"What is she wearing?" Reese asked Jason in a low voice. "That's the longest tunic I've ever seen. Is she even wearing trousers under that?"

"That is what is called a dress or a gown," Jason explained." I've seen them in old Earth images and occasionally at the Earth-reproduction theater at the university, although never one so shiny. Do you think it's made out of foil?"

"I can't tell," she whispered. "I'm blinded by the glare."

Jason chuckled softly.

Maklund walked up to Enberg, smiling like she was meeting an old friend.

"Welcome, Commander. Welcome to all of you."

"Thank you for your hospitality, Madame President," Enberg said, then proceeded to introduce the members of his crew.

President Maklund began to introduce various officials.

"Commander, this is Director Symas Graith. He was the one who first alerted me to your ship's arrival in the solar system. His directorate first spotted your ship."

"I usually just direct our asteroid mining operations," Graith said. "The ship that escorted yours was from my fleet."

"Your asteroid catchers are quite remarkable," Enberg said. "My chief engineer is particularly fascinated by them. She wants to know everything about them."

"That is quite flattering," Graith said, "especially given your ship is far more impressive, crossing interstellar space. I'm curious. What do you use for propulsion?"

"It's a combination of propulsion drives."

"Matter-antimatter?"

"As well as dark energy conversion. Each propulsion system uses a different energy source."

"Please, gentlemen," Maklund said, "let's not devolve into boring tech talk. There's plenty of time for that. Commander, may I introduce Professor Stran Cobler, Senior Academic at Vlaera University, one of our top academic institutions?"

Cobler was shorter than other Spherians, with a pleasantly cherubic face.

"It is a profound pleasure," Cobler said. "In fact, a once-in-a-lifetime opportunity. You see, before I became an administrator I was a history professor. Being present at such a historic meeting is beyond anything I could have ever hoped for."

"Then," Enberg said, "I should introduce you to our historian, Dr. Jason Ford."

"A fellow historian?" Cobler said with excitement, advancing on Jason. "Oh, we have so much to learn from one another."

"I look forward to it," Jason said. "For instance, I'm particularly curious about how your people survived the Great Burning. Frozen embryos raised by robots?"

"Well, the story of robots using ectogenesis to grow embryos is solid and verifiable. Archeologists found the equipment. Our history beyond that is a little fuzzy. There are competing accounts. One says there was a ghost directing the resurrection of humanity. Others say a supreme super-intelligent computer. No evidence has been found for either, especially the ghost." Cobler chuckled. "We believe the first human embryo resurrected was a female named Olivia Price. She then nurtured and led the others that followed. Without her we would not be here."

As Professor Cobler and Jason continued their academic discussion, Nysandra Trin approached Graith.

"What do you think of these Refugians?" she asked.

"Hard to know what to think," Graith murmured.

"Do you think they are working for *them*?"

"I'm not sure," he answered. "I tend to think not. Their bizarre accents. Have you ever heard such an accent anywhere in the SolarSphere?"

"No, but maybe *they* are being clever," she said. "Visitors from another star, that's quite a distraction."

"I have no intention of being distracted," Graith said with an edge in his voice. "If we need to wage a two-front war, so be it."

Eventually, the entire group was guided into another room, which had a large oval table. Everyone was asked to sit. Waiters placed an oval plate in front of each guest. Each plate had nine sections, dividers radiating from the center. Eight of the sections contained a different foodstuff of varying gooeyness. The ninth section was empty.

The crew looked at their plates with curiosity. The Spherians ignored the plates and instead looked at President Maklund.

"I am told by Professor Cobler," the Maklund began, "there is an ancient tradition of short speeches before a meal called a...burn?" Maklund looked to Cobler

"A toast," he corrected.

"A toast," Maklund said, "to the crew of the *Sarania* who have bravely crossed interstellar space to find us. We humbly hope the discovery of our SolarSphere will justify your journey. And may a warm friendship develop."

"Thank you, Madame President," Enberg said. "I'm an explorer, not a diplomat. So my words may not be as eloquent. But please know our discovery of your SolarSphere is far beyond anything we could have expected. I suppose that is the point of exploration. We hope to learn more about our cosmic cousins and the amazing story of your triumph."

"Thank you, Commander, for your kind words," Maklund said. "Please, everyone enjoy your meals and get to know one another."

"Cosmic cousins?" Reese whispered to Jason. "Perhaps we should have brought a speech writer for the Commander."

Jason chuckled softly. "Apparently, no one explained to the Spherians that toasts are given using a drink." Jason squinted at his meal. "Any idea what's on these plates?"

"No idea," Reese whispered back. "Looks like puddings and sauces. Maybe the Spherians have delicate digestive systems."

"Or fragile teeth," Jason said, trying to stifle a chuckle. He watched the Spherians as they began eating using a flat-ended utensil, scraping the various gelatinous mixtures off the plate.

Professor Cobler caught his eye. Jason hoped he hadn't overheard his comment about the food.

"Forgive us," Cobler said at full volume. "We've neglected to explain the significance of our cuisine to our guests. Our host has served the traditional Unity Dish. The eight foodstuffs represent the diverse cultures among the peoples of the SolarSphere. The empty section represents the unknown future and the yet-to-be-added habitats of the SolarSphere."

"Yes," Maklund said, "thank you for pointing this out. This is a dish of greeting. The dish may have different sections, but they are a part of a whole, like the habitats within the SolarSphere. This is often served when one moves to a new biosphere."

"Do people often move between biospheres?" Jason asked.

"It is required that every citizen of the Sphere live in at least five habitats by the time they reach the age of 25. It is so we don't become provincial or isolated in our thinking."

"Ah."

"Pardon me, Commander," Professor Cobler said. "Your ship is called *Sarania*. Is there any significance to that name?"

"Yes, there is actually," Enberg said. "But I'm sure Dr. Ford could tell the story better than I can."

Jason nodded, appreciating Enberg's deference.

"Thank you, Commander." Jason looked forward to giving a lesson to an eager audience for a change. "The Ark that brought our ancestors to Refugia was the brainchild of a man named John Davis."

"Excuse me, what is a *brainchild*?" Cobler asked.

"Ah, sorry," Jason said. "It means it was his invention, his creation. One of the volunteers selected for the Ark mission was a woman named Sarania. It is said that during the preparation period, they fell in love and married. By the time the Ark was ready to launch, Sarania had to stay behind. It is unclear why. Was it an injury? Was she needed to manage ground operations? Many heart-wrenching dramas have been written and suggested the reason why. But they are all speculation.

"What is known is that Davis was devastated. He had to go with the Ark. It was his life's work. However, Sarania Davis did transmit one last message to the Ark, a simple one: 'Save humanity, my love, and report back.' So I suppose, in her absence, we are reporting back. Dear Sarania, thank you for your sacrifice. We made it safe and sound."

The Spherians began softly snapping their fingers. The crew looked around bewildered.

Seeing their confusion, Professor Cobler explained. "It's a form of appreciation. Do you have a similar gesture or ritual?"

"Yes, we clap," Jason answered, "like this."

Jason began to softly clap his fingers against the opposing palm. The others followed.

Grins appeared on the Spherians faces, as some of them began to clap as well.

An aide came to Maklund's side and whispered something in her ear. Her smile faded. She turned to Enberg.

"Commander, I am sorry to interrupt our festivities and good mood. But we have a message from your ship. I'm told there has been an accident."

○ ● ○ ● ○

Trin brought Enberg and Doc Skonauer back to Drydock 168 immediately. The rest of the crew followed in another sliptube capsule.

Once on board, they headed straight for the medical bay. Enberg could see Dr. Srin tending to the unconscious Andy Barosi. Doc pushed past him to work with Srin.

Enberg turned to Covarti, who was standing just inside the medical bay looking devastated.

"What happened?" he asked.

"We were scanning the hull when Andy got hit by one of the rotating spokes on Ring 1. I'm sorry. It's all my fault. If he had been wearing his pressure suit in Earth orbit, according to the mission plan, the suit might have protected him."

"Or the suit might have suffered a rapid decompression," Enberg said, "and killed him. We all accepted the risks of his mission. We'll talk about it later."

Once the rest of the diplomatic party returned to the *Sarania*, the entire crew was briefed on Andy's condition. He had several broken ribs and some internal bleeding. Doc later reported he'd repaired all of Andy's injuries. While in critical condition, he was expected to survive.

The crew had crossed a greater distance than any other humans in history without a single accident. They discovered an unexpected civilization. But now no one was in a celebratory mood. They just milled about outside the sick bay, hoping for more news of Andy's recovery.

Kai Herstonick approached Reese. "Do you have any leftovers? I hate to say it, but that Spherian food was awful."

"Yeah," one of the crew said, "the worst baby food I ever had."

"Eat a lot of baby food, do you?" Kai quipped.

Several others chuckled. The comment was perfect for breaking the tension.

"Yeah, what the heck was that stuff?" Jason asked.

"Well, I expect to find out," Reese said, pulling some small vials out of her pockets. "I took some samples."

"In front of the Spherians?" Jason asked.

"I was discreet," she answered, grinning. "Now anyone who wants leftovers, follow me."

○ ● ○ ● ○

Roughly an hour after the crew's sudden departure, Symas Graith walked into Maklund's office.

"Madame President," Graith said, "First Minister Trin mentioned you are contemplating giving these Refugians free run of the Sphere."

"I am considering many things," Maklund said, not looking up from her reports.

"Do you think it wise?"

"I have my reasons. And I understand your concern," Maklund said, expecting Graith's inherent paranoia.

"I'm not sure you do," Graith said. "These seemingly friendly explorers could actually be a reconnaissance force. They say our presence was unexpected. But that may be a ruse."

Maklund finally looked up from her reports.

"It took them four years to cross interstellar space," she said in a tone as if speaking to a child. "I may not be an expert on invasions, but wouldn't that be the slowest invasion in human history?"

"But what if they are lying about the time it took to arrive?" Graith asked. "Or what if there is an armada just beyond the Oort cloud?"

"We still saw them coming weeks before they arrived at the Sphere, thanks to your team's vigilance. And if they are indeed enemies, why offer to have us board their vessel?"

"Board their vessel?" Graith asked. "When was this offer made?"

"Just as Enberg was leaving during the dinner," Maklund said. "To return the hospitality. Why else?"

"Perhaps to take you hostage?" Graith suggested.

"Enough! I appreciate your caution, but it borders on paranoia. Their explanation makes perfect sense. Their invitation is simply to reciprocate. Besides, your people control the drydock. I assume you have had your people analyze their vessel."

"Yes," Graith said. "I've assigned a team, including Dr. Theris from Vlaera."

"Good. Plus, they can't leave with the bay doors closed."

"Yes, that's true," he conceded. "But what happens after they have taken in all the Sphere has to offer?"

"They want to go to Earth," Maklund said, "poke around, take its temperature and go home."

"Landing on Earth is illegal."

"Yes, for us," Maklund said. "But do our laws apply to them?"

"Earth is within the SolarSphere, It's within our territory."

"A legal case could be made that our laws only apply to the inhabitants of the Sphere. We abandoned Earth and therefore it is open to salvage."

"Earth is not some derelict asteroid catcher!"

Maklund laughed. "Some might say that is exactly what it is."

She finally stood up and looked Graith in the eye. "What on Earth are you so afraid of?"

Chapter 6

Reese Monsell was working at a frenzied pace. She had been generally happy to feed her crew during the last four years. It was challenging and fulfilling to change up the menu, particularly after a twist. But to feed a head of state that might have different dietary needs and expectations made Reese extremely apprehensive. She had inquired about any dietary restrictions the Spherians might have, but First Minister Trin said there were none. But Reese didn't trust that, given what she saw at their welcome dinner.

Should I overcook the vegetables to make them softer for the Spherians? She hated overcooked vegetables.

"Grig," she called out. "Where are the rest of those wipper beans? I need more for the hearth stew."

"I asked Corson to bring more from the Ring 4 garden half an hour ago," Grig answered.

"What is he doing, a tour of the rings?" Reese snapped.

Jason walked into the galley. Grig rolled his eyes in exasperation as he passed. Obviously, Reese was not handling the pressure well, taking it out on those assigned to help her. Usually, she was the calming influence. But not today.

"Can I help in any way?" Jason asked.

"I just hope I don't poison them all," Reese fretted as she was coordinating the food preparation.

"Don't worry," Jason said. "The Spherians didn't poison us, well, not really."

"I never expected to cater a diplomatic event. I haven't even had time to complete the analysis on their baby food."

"Relax. The Commander said they insisted on trying our cuisine. They understand it won't be the same as their pudding-like food."

"Yeah, but no one will blame *him* if they break a tooth on the croutons."

Jason burst out laughing. "Be on guard, Spherians," he chuckled. "She's carrying a lethal crouton, and she knows how to use it!"

Looking perplexed, Corson, who had just entered, dropped the basket and exited quickly. They both continued to laugh as Corson scurried out.

Reese hugged Jason. "Thanks, I needed that," she whispered.

"You'll be fine," Jason reassured her. "What's the worst that could happen?"

"Interstellar war?"

○ ● ○ ● ○

An hour later, Jason, Enberg, Lyla and a few others watched their guests arrive through the viewports. The platform in Drydock 168 began extending with President Maklund and her party on it.

"That's much more dignified than crossing with a rope line," Jason mumbled to himself.

This time President Maklund wore no gown, an impractical garment for zero-G. Yet, her burgundy pantsuit was just as elegant, just less glaring. She was accompanied by Symas Graith, Nysandra Trin, Professor Cobler and the ever-recording Glynn.

Jason noticed Graith surveying the length of *Sarania*'s exterior, soaking in every detail of the vessel.

He's the one to watch, Jason thought.

He and Enberg moved toward to airlock to greet their guests.

Glynn entered *Sarania*'s airlock first, then turned around to record Maklund's entrance, ignoring the crew. Jason noted the irony that Glynn was the first Spherian to ever enter a Refugian ship, yet he seemed oblivious to this historic event and was more interested in the President's entrance than the people from another star floating next to him.

"Welcome on board the *Sarania*," said Enberg, as Maklund entered. "I'll be honest, our mission plan never included entertaining guests so please excuse the cramped quarters."

"Thank you, Commander," she said. "Your ship looks charming."

Jason smiled at that comment. He didn't think charming was what the designers had in mind.

"Cramped? To the contrary," said Graith, who was floating behind Maklund. "Your ship appears quite roomy. Spacious when compared to our asteroid catchers."

"Commander," Maklund said, "before we go on I must ask, how is your injured crewmember doing?"

"He's recovering, but needs rest. So he won't be joining us this evening."

"I understand. Please give my best wishes for a quick recovery."

"Thank you. I will." Then Enberg gestured them all toward the zero-G central core to the spoke hatches to Ring 2. The two hatch openings, each on opposite sides, were rotating around the central core.

"Impressive," Graith said, looking around. "I expect the *Sarania* is the pride of your fleet."

Enberg frowned. "I'm afraid there is no fleet. The *Sarania* is a one-mission ship, one of a kind. Once we return to Refugia, the *Sarania* will be the first vessel to cross interplanetary space and return home."

"What about your Ark?" Graith asked.

"The Ark only traveled one way. *Sarania* will make a round trip." Enberg turned back to President Maklund. "Now, if you'll just climb down, following Dr. Covarti," he said, gesturing to Lyla floating at the hatch to the spoke tunnel.

Lyla grabbed the handhold and maneuvered her body through the hatch feet first.

"Just make sure to hold tight to the ladder as you descend," Lyla explained. She then disappeared down the tunnel.

Maklund waved Graith on to proceed ahead of her. Graith had more experience with this type of gravitational transition during his years on asteroid catchers. He maneuvered easily into the spoke tunnel, although not as gracefully as Lyla. Maklund turned to Glynn, waving a finger to indicate this was not to be recorded. After she attempted the maneuver herself, imperfectly but successfully, the others followed.

Once the entire party climbed down to the artificial gravity afforded by the rotating ring deck, Maklund and her party seemed to relax, with the possible exception of Graith. Jason suspected he never relaxed.

"Madame President," Enberg said, "I believe you've met Dr. Monsell, our chief biologist. She also has served as our head chef, keeping us well-fed and sane throughout our journey."

"Good evening, Madame President," Reese said. "On the *Sarania*, we are not set up for formal dining. However, we thought a buffet might allow you to try a variety of our dishes. After dinner we'd like to offer you a tour of the ship."

"That's very gracious of you," Maklund said. "I do have one question: What is a buffet?"

"The buffet table to our right is set with a variety of serving dishes. The guests fill their plates with whichever foods appeal to them or sample whichever ones they'd like to try. I thought since our cuisine would be new to you, it would be a way for you to sample more than one dish."

"Think of it as our version of the Unity Dish," Jason added.

"How thoughtful." Maklund smiled, seeming genuinely pleased.

"This first dish is called hearth stew, a favorite from the northern regions of Refugia, particularly during winter."

"What is winter?" Maklund asked. "One of your holidays?"

Some of the crew chuckled, but Enberg gave them a harsh stare. "It's a planetary season, usually colder than the other seasons," he explained.

"After that," Reese continued, "we have tomato pie, broccoli balls in bean curd, a potato and mushroom soufflé, spirulina and carrot clusters, wipper dumplings and finally stem steak in a golden marinade sauce."

"We have tomatoes and carrots but not exactly like these," Maklund said, holding up a spherical carrot. She politely took a small sample of each dish. On the other hand, Professor Cobler, fascinated by the offerings, packed his plate. Once everyone had filled their plates, they all sat at the dining table.

"I suppose it's my turn to offer an opening toast," Enberg said, standing and picking up his glass. "On Refugia, we offer a toast using a beverage. Both our ancestors overcame amazing odds to ensure humanity's survival, each in different but noble and courageous ways. We, the descendants of John Davis, welcome and toast the descendants of Olivia Price."

Enberg raised his glass higher. The crew did as well. The Spherian guests mimicked their actions. Enberg then drank. The others followed his lead.

"Enberg's toasts are getting better," Reese whispered to Jason. "Did you help him?"

"A little bit," he whispered back.

Maklund gave a toast similar to the one she made at their previous dinner, which was followed by a combination of snapping and clapping, after which individual conversations broke out.

"Excuse me, Commander," Trin said. "May I ask, what was it like growing up on a planet? I mean, never having to worry about bone density loss or radiation levels."

"Well, I admit I never worried about those things until I joined the Space Administration. Before that I worried mostly about the fireweed."

"Fireweed?"

"Yes," Enberg said. "I'm sure Dr. Monsell could explain the science better than I can. Reese?"

"Yes, thank you," Reese said, not expecting to be at the center of the conversation after the food was served. "When our ancestors settled on Refugia, there were already some indigenous plants on the planet. Not all the plants brought from Earth on the Ark could grow in the Refugian soil. A few of the indigenous plants were edible, but most were not very palatable. Wipper beans and queelnuts were notable exceptions. Our botanists tried to develop hybrid strains to make farmland agriculture possible. They were somewhat successful."

"'Somewhat' suggests a problem," Maklund said

"Yes, there were some great successes, like queelnuts" Reese, said, nodding her head. "However, a strain of kale spliced together with a native plant also thrived. But it thrived too well. Our farmers rejoiced at first. But we soon discovered it was quite an invasive species and very difficult to eradicate. Usually burning is needed, thus the name fireweed." Reese looked to Enberg. "Every Refugian is required to perform a two-year stint with the fireweeders. Some are born into the fireweeder families and spend their lives burning this incredible scourge."

"If it was edible and an agricultural success," Professor Cobler asked, "why is it now a scourge?"

"Once fireweed grows in an area, that soil becomes unusable for any other plants. It excretes a mild toxin, harmless to humans, but toxic to most crops. So the plant and the soil must be burned to eradicate the plant and the toxins."

"And some people spend their entire lives burning these weeds?" Cobler asked.

"Yes," Enberg said. "I myself was born into a fireweeder family. We lived on what is called the Outer Scorch. It appears once again humanity has severely damaged a planetary ecosystem. First, the Great Burning of Earth, and now another type of burning—this time on Refugia."

"Is that why you came in search of Earth?" Graith asked. "To see if your people could return?"

Enberg smiled. "Our mission has three primary objectives. First, evaluate the twist drive. Second, discover what happened to Earth. And third and last, determine if the Earth remained close to habitable. I'll admit the fireweed is a challenge. However, there is no way for our entire population to immigrate back to Earth. We simply don't have the resources to transport 300 million people. One of the many questions this expedition seeks to answer is whether it would be possible for a smaller group of colonists to make a reasonable attempt at returning to ensure the survival of our species, should the conditions on Refugia deteriorate."

"The conditions on Earth are not survivable," Professor Cobler said. "I can assure you we would have returned if it were otherwise. That's why landings on Earth are illegal."

Maklund and Graith shot each other looks of concern.

Graith turned to Trin. "Was Cobler not briefed?" he whispered to her.

"I suppose not well enough," she answered.

"Well," Enberg said, "that question is now moot."

"Why is it moot?" Maklund asked.

"You all," Enberg said. "The SolarSphere. Humanity will survive, regardless of whatever happens on Refugia. And that's wonderful news."

Jason watched the Spherians as the conversation continued. Maklund was polite and tasted everything but barely. Cobler relished his food, contemplating each bite.

Graith had taken little on his plate, and barely noticed it, focusing more on the people at the table.

Once they had finished their meal, Enberg gave their guests a tour of *Sarania*. First, they toured the rings. Reese was able to brag about her gardens which took up 70 percent of the ring space. Then Lyla provided a tour of the engineering section.

"I was wondering," Cobler asked, "why is your propulsion system called a twist drive? Why not a warp drive? It does warp space-time, correct?"

"Yes, it does," Lyla answered, "but imperfectly. Dark matter distorts that warping. It *twists* our course. That is one of the reasons it took us four years to arrive here. But we've mapped quite a bit of the dark matter along the way."

"So your return trip should be much quicker?"

"Unfortunately not," Lyla said. "The universe is expanding so Refugia is farther away now. While navigation will be improved, the distance will be significantly longer. It's a trade-off. We still expect at least a four-year return voyage. Then we'll get to explore another new world."

"I'm not sure I follow," Cobler said.

"While there is no time dilation during the twist themselves, the time and distance between twists do suffer from some time dilation. We estimate we'll return roughly 120 years after we left Refugia."

"In that time," Jason continued, "everyone we knew will have died. In fact, many are already dead. Scientific advances will have been made. The government may have changed. Certainly, there will be social changes."

"So," Maklund said, "you've sacrificed a lot to travel here."

"Yes," Enberg said solemnly. "But finding the SolarSphere has made it worthwhile. And that's just the beginning."

"Well, Commander," Maklund said, "you've given us a lot to think about. I thank you for your hospitality."

"Before you go we have a gift." Enberg said, turning to Jason. "Dr. Ford?"

Jason brought over a small metallic box. Jason opened it to reveal an object Maklund did not seem to recognize.

"It's a book," Cobler said excitedly. "An old-fashioned book with paper pages."

"It is a replica of the Refugian Charter as written by John Davis."

"We were going to leave it on Earth," Enberg said, "preferably at Sarania Davis's grave, should we be able to find it."

"We hope," Jason added, "by reading it you will come to know more about us."

○ ● ○ ● ○

Preldon Krelnikoff decompressed the airlock on the edge of Sector L. Once the air had been evacuated, he pressed the buttons to open the hatch. Because he was "spacewalking"—as the ancient cosmonauts called it—on the sun side or interior of the sphere, his pressure suit had extra radiation shielding. This made it bulkier, but he didn't mind.

Krelnikoff was descended from Russian oligarchs, ones rich enough to have their embryos frozen before the Great Burning. Beyond that he knew nothing of them. However, as an Earth history buff, he preferred to identify with the earliest Russian cosmonauts, men who ventured into space with far less protection than he had. He was unusual for a Spherian in that he actually had an interest in Earth before the Great Burning. However, his true love was spacewalking.

He had these thoughts every time he pressure-suited into space. But now he had to focus on his mission. Maintenance was his official assignment. He would report perfect structural integrity regardless of what he found in this older section of the Sphere. Actually, structural flaws would be an advantage, making the job of placing his explosives easier.

He maneuvered to an obsolete thruster port, which provided an ideal structural vulnerability and an easy hiding place for the explosive package. He placed three more packages in similar hiding places.

Suddenly, something grabbed his arm from behind, completely immobilizing it. He used the zero-G to rotate his body around. Before he could make sense of what he was seeing, something claw-like moved past his visor and punctured his suit. His visor fogged up before he lost consciousness.

CHAPTER 7

Brother Yurasti reviewed the latest round of reports. One, in particular, disturbed him. It was not public yet, but his source was reliable. President Maklund was about to announce the arrival of the Refugians to the general population. It was inevitable. What upset him more was that Maklund was considering giving these outsiders complete freedom to explore the SolarSphere. It was a complication for which Yurasti could not quite calculate the effects.

The door signal beeped. It would be Maynberc, punctual as ever.

"President Maklund is planning to give the Refugians unfettered access to the Sphere. Can you believe it? The woman is an idiot." Suddenly, Yurasti felt a twinge of embarrassment for his eruption. "Forgive me my outburst, Brother Maynberc."

"I presume she does not understand the ramifications."

Yurasti had to admit to the logic of what Maynberc said. He tried to imagine what he might do in her place without the information Yurasti's organization possessed.

"Master, I bring more significant news. Preldon Krelnikoff has disappeared. He did not check in after his last mission. No one reports seeing him."

Yurasti's stomach turned unpleasantly. Several possible ramifications ran through his brain.

"I assume he has not been detained by any authorities," he said. "And that an accident has been ruled out?"

"Both were ruled out. My investigation was thorough."

"Of course, it was." Yurasti knew Maynberc's work was always complete.

"The only logical conclusion is that he's been captured by *them*." Yurasti sighed. "Of course, Krelnikoff will resist revealing his mission."

"He still might, if forced."

Yurasti had to agree. No one knew what *they* were capable of more than Maynberc.

"Krelnikoff will try to kill himself before revealing anything, provided he is afforded the opportunity." Yurasti mourned Krelnikoff. He was dedicated to the cause. And despite working at such a sobering profession, he had a lively, joyous spirit. Regardless of what happened, that would be gone.

Yurasti had to refocus himself. "Are the explosives he set still in place?"

"Yes," Maynberc said. "It's unlikely they have discovered his mission, at least not yet."

Yurasti looked from Maynberc to his control panel. "We may have to accelerate our timetable."

○ ● ○ ● ○

Enberg was in the ship's mess, finishing his breakfast. Jason approached his table.

"Commander, do you have a moment?"

"Of course, Jason," he said, scraping the last food off his plate. "What's on your mind?"

"A comment Professor Cobler made last night," Jason said, as he sat down across the table.

"About landings on Earth being illegal?"

Jason nodded his head.

"Yeah, I've been thinking about that all morning," Enberg said.

"So have the crew. Obviously, it's of great concern."

"You mean in regard to the Contract?"

"More than the Contract," Jason said. "Surveying Earth is our whole mission. Do you think the Spherians would really prevent us from going to Earth?"

"I don't know. I'm not sure they've decided themselves. You caught the alarmed looks Maklund and Graith shot each other?"

"Yes, they didn't look too pleased with Professor Cobler. Maklund works so hard to be so gracious, but I think we saw a crack in her diplomatic façade."

Enberg nodded in agreement, looking down into his mug. "Hypothetically—putting the Contract aside for a moment—do you think discovering the SolarSphere was worth the trip?"

"The SolarSphere is amazing and definitely worth exploring." Jason leaned back in his chair, pondering the implication of Enberg's question. "Commander, have you ever heard of the Holy Grail?"

"No."

"In ancient Earth mythology, it was an elusive object of great value. It was the subject of great quests, and some even say wars. Some were said to devote their entire lives to finding it."

"What did this grail thing do?"

"The stories vary. An instrument of healing? A weapon of great power? A door to great wisdom? All depending on the account."

"Sounds useful," Enberg said. "Did anyone ever find it?"

"Again, the legends vary. But my point is Earth is *our* Holy Grail. And we are so close."

"I may have made a mistake in allowing them to close the drydock doors," Enberg admitted. "We can't leave until they open them."

"You think they would actually prevent us from leaving?" Enberg shrugged.

○ ● ○ ● ○

Enberg requested a meeting with President Maklund. She agreed quite quickly, almost as if she were expecting the need to meet. Enberg entered the President's office, expecting her aides and entourage, which she usually had. Instead, the President of the SolarSphere was alone.

"Welcome, Commander."

"Thank you for seeing me, Madame President."

"My pleasure," Maklund said. "Let me ask you, when you came to dinner the other night, did anyone show you the Spherical Council Chamber?"

"I don't believe so."

"Oh, that's right," Maklund said. "You had to leave to tend to your injured crew member. How is he doing?"

"Well," Enberg said, "our doctor tells me he is recovering nicely."

"Good. Let me give you a quick tour of the Spherical Council Chamber. It's just through this door."

Maklund opened a large door and held it open for Enberg. He walked through into a dark chamber. As he entered, the lights brightened, slowly revealing an enormous auditorium, a far larger room than he had ever seen. He estimated there were well over 10,000 seats.

"We are a republic. The Spherical Council, our legislative body, meets for 10 days out of 50."

"That doesn't seem like very much."

"Really?" Maklund said. "Well, it takes several days to travel from the far side of the SolarSphere. We were in the final day of our last session when I was alerted to *Sarania*'s presence. Symas Graith alerted me at that very desk."

"Did you tell the members of the Council?" Enberg asked.

"No, it was early days. You and I hadn't even spoken yet. We didn't even know if you were human. There was no reason to panic the billions of people in the Sphere. But I'll be making an announcement soon."

"Billions? Exactly how many people live in the SolarSphere?"

"Over 23 billion."

"Wow." He looked out at the cavernous room. "And each member of your Council represents one of your cylindrical biospheres?"

Maklund chuckled. "No, we don't have enough seats for that. Each councilor usually represents a sector of biospheres."

Instead of returning to her office, Maklund sat down in the front row and gestured for Enberg to do likewise. It seemed strange for two people alone to share such a massive chamber for a private conversation.

"I suspect you didn't come here today to discuss our political system."

"No."

"What's on your mind, Commander?"

"Earth," he said. "Apparently, it is illegal to land on Earth?"

Maklund gave a taut smile.

"Yes, I'm afraid Professor Cobler wasn't very discreet. I'm sorry about that. Your desire to land on Earth has been of some discussion in legal and political circles. That's why I haven't mentioned it."

"Please understand, we're simply explorers."

"But historically," Maklund said, "exploration often leads to colonization."

"We have no interest in staking any claim to Earth."

"I didn't think so, but the precedent worries some people. However, that's not the main issue."

"Then, what is?"

"The last landing on Earth—approximately 50 years ago—was disastrous. An entire crew was lost. The rescue mission was equally disastrous. So, it is a safety issue. Apparently, the planet has become geologically unstable, something called planetary quakes. The atmosphere is not only unbreathable, it has become extremely—what was the term, ah yes—*turbulent*. Are you familiar with the term?"

"Yes," Enberg said. "As a pilot, I'm quite familiar with turbulence."

"I wasn't, not until I received my first briefing on the matter, some years ago. As you can imagine, we don't have a lot of wind on the SolarSphere."

Enberg smiled.

"Believe it or not," he said, "we are prepared for such a situation. We've trained on Refugia for turbulent landings."

"But if you ran into trouble," Maklund said, "wouldn't it be natural to call for help?"

"We would not ask any citizen of the SolarSphere to endanger themselves rescuing us." Enberg decided to test Maklund's reaction to a challenge. "And there is a question of whether you have the legal authority to stop us."

"Yes," Maklund answered, seeming to take no offense. "And thus, the discussions among our legal experts."

Enberg leaned forward. "Why does it matter to your government what risks we take?"

"Because others will want to take the risk as well," Maklund said. "Are you familiar with the concept of smuggling?"

"Yes," Enberg said.

"There are still resources on Earth that would be useful to some SolarSphere endeavors, but now the risk is too high. We've been fairly successful in discouraging Earth salvage in the last few decades. However, if you successfully land on Earth, that might spur new attempts at illegal scavenging. People more poorly trained than your crew may die."

Enberg sighed at hearing this.

"I understand your position," he said. "We also have a legal issue, something called the Contract. As was mentioned at dinner, everyone we know on Refugia will be dead by the time we return. Even our skills will likely be obsolete. So future employment will likely be difficult. To compensate, we are to be paid handsomely upon the completion of our mission. Currency has been placed in a trust for the crew. But the primary stipulation is that we actually land on Earth and show proof. At the end of our mission, that trust will be all we have in a world that may have moved on significantly."

"I see," she said, "an economic incentive."

"I know it may seem petty in the light of the great discoveries we've made and still hope to make."

"No, I understand your position," Maklund said. "Perhaps, I can offer you an alternative, a solution you wouldn't have ordinarily considered. So far you've only visited the docking bay and GovCenter, correct?"

"So far," Enberg agreed.

"I'd like to show you another habitat, if you have the time. It's one of our newest."

"I'd be honored."

Nysandra Trin accompanied Maklund and Enberg in a sliptube capsule.

"Madame President," Trin said, "you realize this is not an operational habitat."

"Yes, I know."

Enberg could see whatever Maklund was up to was confusing for Trin.

They traveled to the sliptube station and settled into the capsule. Maklund punched in the coordinates herself.

"This should take less than an hour. In the meantime I have a question: Why did you volunteer to command the *Sarania*? I mean personally, beyond the glory and the adventure."

"That's a long story I suppose."

"Longer than the time we have in this capsule?"

"I suppose not." He smiled. "As you've learned, I was raised in a fireweeder family. My father even took me along on minor burn runs, nothing too dangerous for my age. But I knew where my life was headed. When I was young, my parents were given a month's leave. They decided to take me to Davis Heights, one of our major cities. It was frightening at first but also magical for a nine-year-old. So many unfamiliar sights.

"One day, we went to the Earth Museum. I had heard of Earth, of course, but never thought too much about it. In the museum's auditorium, they showed a video that had footage from Earth, footage that was over 2000 years old. It was part of the Ark Records."

"I'd love to see some of that footage," Maklund said.

"I'm sure Jason can provide it. Of all the images I recall, what I remember most was the footage where the camera was mounted on a bird."

"What's a bird?"

"I didn't know either," Enberg said. "We don't have them on Refugia, but they were small animals that instead of arms had wings. They could actually fly in a planet's atmosphere just by flapping their wings. As I said the camera was mounted on the bird. The video was incredible. It was like we were flying with the bird. At that moment I fell in love with flying.

"After our vacation, we returned to the Outer Scorch. As expected, I eventually enlisted as a fireweeder. I did a fair number of burn runs. Then I volunteered for training in the Air Corps. I found I really loved flying. Mostly I just transported fireweeders to the front for burn runs. A glorified transport driver."

"But somehow," Maklund surmised, "you distinguished yourself."

"Yes. We received a report that fireweed had infiltrated a tall geological structure called the Red Tower. It was growing its way up the rockfaces. The Tower is adjacent to the Red Cliffs area. The commanders were perplexed about how to burn the fireweed in an area only accessible by mountain climbers. There was no way anyone could carry enough accelerant that high, plus the danger to anyone who tried.

"I came up with a lunatic idea to mount flame guns on my copter, wiring them so I could trigger them from the cockpit. The commanders let me try it. And it worked. I initiated the first aerial assault on fireweed.

"It took days, but I turned the Red Tower almost completely black. Afterward, I decided to land on the top where the fireweed hadn't quite made it, the one part that was still red. I felt like I was on top of the world. I suppose I was. Then I looked down. And I saw a worm wiggled out of a crevice, a type I had never seen before. There's very little animal life on Refugia. As I looked at this worm, I saw little appendages. They almost looked like wings. In that moment, I was that nine-year-old boy again. Were these vestigial wings? Was this species evolving wings? I supposed I'll never know."

"So," Maklund said, "you crossed interstellar space in search of birds?"

Enberg laughed. "That and the adventure and glory."

After a few more minutes, they arrived at their destination.

"This habitat is well above the orbital plane," Maklund said. "On the edge of our expansion."

They exited the sliptube capsule.

"Nysandra, I'd like to escort Commander Enberg down alone."

"Are you sure?"

Maklund responded with silence.

"I'll wait here, Madame President," Trin said.

Enberg followed Maklund into the elevator. This elevator was dropping more quickly than the one in GovCenter.

"I'd like to offer you an alternate solution to our problem," Maklund said, "one you wouldn't have ordinarily considered."

"And what would that be?"

At that moment the doors opened, and Maklund walked out.

What is she playing at? he wondered.

Curious, he followed her. For a second he felt disoriented. The vastness of a seeming void overwhelmed him. Then his eyes adjusted. It was another habitat. He guessed it was the same size of the GovCenter habitat, but was completely empty and devoid of any significant detail. He was finally able to focus on a large case in front of them, probably left behind by workers.

"This habitat was completed and pressurized almost a year ago," Maklund said.

"Then where are the buildings and other structures?"

"Once the residents are chosen, they will decide on the architecture." Maklund stepped closer. "Or….this could be *your* habitat."

"Excuse me?"

"Stay here, here on the SolarSphere," she said. "We could give you and your crew your own habitat. Perhaps even a seat on the Council. Become one of us."

Enberg stepped back, trying to comprehend this unexpected offer.

"That's a generous proposal," he said. "Incredibly generous. You'd do this, just to avoid having us land on Earth?"

"Not just that," Maklund said. "You may be able to help us solve one of our own problems. We are facing a crisis of our own, perhaps not as dramatic as your fireweed, but a crisis all the same."

"What sort of crisis?" Enberg asked.

Maklund stepped away from him. The expression on her face made Enberg think she was unsure of what she was about to say. She sat down on the case left behind by the workers.

"What I'm about to share with you is highly confidential," she said in a low voice. "Only a small group of key scientists know about this. Some would be horrified that I am sharing it with someone who has no loyalty to the SolarSphere. Can I trust you to keep this secret?"

"As long as it doesn't endanger my crew or our mission."

She nodded. "As you have learned, our ancestors were descended from frozen embryos, specifically 723 embryos. The problem is that many of those embryos were siblings. There were actually only 149 sibling groups. So our population lacks sufficient genetic diversity."

"I'm not a biologist," Enberg said, "so I'm not sure I understand the issue."

"The lack of genetic diversity means that recessive traits, specifically genetic diseases, are more likely. This, combined with prolonged radiation exposure in the early years of the SolarSphere, created an increased likelihood of genetic diseases. One particular concern is something called Meltron's Syndrome. One of the effects of Meltron's is sterility."

"I'm so sorry," Enberg said.

"It's not an immediately apparent crisis. But our population numbers are beginning to level off. We've downplayed the trend. Our scientists believe we may start to see a population decline within a generation. After that, a population collapse. Within a century it could cause our extinction."

"But you said a moment ago, the SolarSphere had a population of over 23 billion."

"It wouldn't matter if we had a trillion if they were mostly sterile."

"But they're not all sterile, are they?"

"No, but enough are sterile or have a low enough fertility rate to trigger a population collapse. While life expectancy has increased, infant mortality rates have also increased. Such a collapse will begin with a shortage of younger people, those who are the most productive and creative. A shortage of younger people with a relative overage of older people will rip our social structures apart."

"I'm sorry to hear that," Enberg said, still unsure of where this revelation was leading.

"One possible solution is an infusion of new and diverse DNA. If you and your crew stay and interbreed with our population, you could help alleviate the entire crisis. You could be our saviors. And think of the size farm Dr. Monsell could build here. And not a single sprig of fireweed to be found!"

Enberg scowled.

"Sorry. Am I overselling it?" Maklund asked. "But we would compensate you quite generously, possibly beyond what your Contract might offer."

"That would mean abandoning our mission," Enberg said.

"I don't expect an immediate answer. But I ask that you consider it. I trust you will restrict the information I've shared to your crew. I ask they be discreet. In the meantime, I invite you to explore the habitats of our SolarSphere freely. But, as you do, think of what a fulfilling life you and your crew could build here."

"Well, Madame President, you've given me a lot to think about."

"Let me give you one more thing to ponder." Maklund opened her bag and pulled out the copy of the Refugian Charter she had received the night before and opened it to a bookmarked page. She began to read. "Article 4. 'Give aid to your brethren for you are your brethren.'" Maklund then looked up at Enberg. "Your John Davis was a wise man."

Enberg smiled. "You're not the first to use the words of John Davis to manipulate people."

"Manipulate? I prefer the term *persuade*. People often dismiss politicians as self-serving manipulators. Yes, I'm a politician, but a desperate one, desperate to save my people."

○ ● ○ ● ○

The following day President Maklund announced the arrival of the Refugians to the entire population of the SolarSphere and granted the crew of the *Sarania* complete access to all the departments and biospheres of the SolarSphere.

Enberg and his crew were eager to take advantage of this new open-door policy. He also shared Maklund's offer of permanent residence, as well as the reason behind it. All agreed to keep this information to themselves.

They worked out a rotating schedule so the *Sarania* was never unmanned. In an unexpected turn, Lyla Covarti requested permission to join Captain Torg's ship on an asteroid-catching mission, which would take several days.

After their last planning meeting concluded, Jason teased, "Lyla, you're always the contrarian."

"I'm not a contrarian," Lyla said. "It's just that I don't always go with the herd. There's a difference. You're all going to the Sphere. I've seen the sliptubes and visited a biosphere. They're amazing."

"I'm sure there's a lot more to see," Jason said.

"I'm sure there is," Lyla said. "And you'll all record it and write wonderful reports, but— What was that ancient Earth poem you talked about? The one about walking in the wilderness?"

Jason had to think a moment to recall. "*The Road Not Taken*?" he asked.

"Yeah, that's the one," she said.

"Funny. Of all my lectures that's the thing you remember?"

"What can I say? It spoke to me." Lyla said. "Anyway, I have to go pack my bag."

"I still think you're a contrarian."

"Whatever."

Before she left Lyla and some of the other engineers set up a connection between their communication system and that of the SolarSphere, making it easier to coordinate the comings and goings of the crew.

Doctors Skonauer and Srin would take turns rotating through the Sphere's top medical facility. They still had Andy Barosi to look after.

Professor Cobler extended an invitation to the entire crew to visit Vlaera University. Jason and Reese would be the first to visit. Cobler met them at the sliptube station nearest the drydock.

"Isn't Commander Enberg coming?" Cobler asked.

"He may join us later," Jason said. "He's been asked to meet with a few members of the Spherical Council."

"Ah, well then, let me present you with your passkeys. They are required to operate the sliptube system." Cobler handed one small cylindrical object to each of them. "President Maklund, giving you access to the SolarSphere would be pointless without passkeys. I'll demonstrate how to use them as we head to Vlaera."

They entered the sliptube capsule. Cobler gestured they sit in the front seats as he sat in the second row.

"Just insert your passkey into the port, then select from the destination menu."

Jason found Vlaera on the menu and tapped the selection on the screen for Vlaera University.

"Now press the execute bar at the bottom of the screen," Cobler instructed.

As soon as he did, acceleration began. A time counter began, automatically indicating the journey should take 54 minutes.

"The time will vary depending on the traffic patterns and volume. We will pass through 117 biospheres on the way."

"Can we see them as we're passing through?" Reese asked.

"I'm afraid not," Cobler said. "We'll pass through too quickly. However, once we arrive, we have scheduled a reception in your honor. I think you'll find the cuisine at the university far more interesting than the bland Unity Dish at GovCenter."

Both Jason and Reese burst out laughing.

"It was awful, wasn't it?" Cobler asked, smiling. "You'll find every biosphere or habitat has a different culture. Some are quite eccentric."

He turned to Reese. "As a biologist, I think you'll also find our farming methods interesting. Almost every habitat has a farm, providing food and oxygen. In fact, we have one biosphere, not far from the university, that has a tree over 100 kilometers tall."

"Oh, I've got to see that," Reese said, grinning.

After some more small talk, they arrived at the university's station. They approached the elevator. The elevator walls were transparent, unlike the one at GovCenter. As they descended and the artificial gravity began to assert itself, Jason and Reese could observe the campus of Vlaera University getting closer. The cylindrical space was breathtakingly large; it almost made Jason agoraphobic.

"How far down do we have to go?" Reese asked.

"Only about 125 kilometers," Cobler said. "Nothing at all compared to the millions of kilometers we've already traveled."

Reese recalled Lyla's estimate of the size of the habitats. *She was right on.*

Reese and Jason kept their faces pressed to the window.

"Amazing," Jason murmured. "Far more elegant than GovCenter."

Eventually, they reached the bottom. The elevator doors opened into a small park with lawns, gardens and trees. Once they passed through a large arch to the main campus, they found themselves in front of a large statue.

"Wow," Reese said. "I wouldn't have expected a stone statue in space. I would have thought the weight of the stone would have been prohibitive."

"First, we're not *in space*. What a strange idea," Cobler said. "Second, the statue is not stone. It is made of a fabricated polymer, produced in microscopic layers."

"That's Olivia Price, isn't it?" observed Jason.

"Yes," Cobler said with a tone of respect, "stepmother to us all."

Jason strained to make sense of the statue. The front was straightforward, a figure of a young woman holding an infant in each arm. However, behind the form of Olivia Price was a transparent figure, constructed of glass, plastic or some similar material. The features of the second figure were not distinct.

"Who or what is the figure behind Price?" Jason asked.

"Ah, that is Redstone, the great historical enigma," Cobler said. "According to various legends, Olivia Price had a mentor."

"But I thought Price was the first embryo successfully resurrected by robots."

"Yes, all the historical accounts seem consistent on that point. However, certain accounts indicate she had a mentor of some sort. Some say it was an artificially intelligent robot, which is the most likely. Yet, other records suggest it was the ghost of a woman who died centuries before. Others say it was something called an angel. We're not sure what an angel is, so Redstone remains a bit of a mystery."

This was the same story Cobler told at dinner.

"History is always a tapestry of imperfect information," Jason said.

"So true," Cobler agreed.

Chapter 8

Lyla Covarti arrived at the docking port to join the crew of Asteroid Catcher 1065, the same craft that escorted the *Sarania* to the SolarSphere. Before arriving she was given a pair of shoes with triangular nobs on the bottom. She noticed the knob fit neatly into triangular holes in the deck. It enabled one to lock one's foot into the deck plating. *Ingenious.*

She found a young man who was also waiting at the docking port.

"Are you with the asteroid catcher?" she asked.

"I'm Cadet Brall Traskin. I've been assigned to the 1065 as my first tour of duty." He looked nervous. "You're not with the Catcher Corps, are you?"

"No, I'm Dr. Lyla Covarti, the chief engineer of the *Sarania*. But please, call me Lyla."

"You can call me Brall." He had a puzzled look on his face. "What is the *Sarania*?"

"My spaceship. From Refugia."

The puzzled look transformed into a shocked expression.

"Oh, you're one of the aliens?"

Lyla chuckled. "I've never been called an alien before. You do realize I'm human just like you."

"I guess so. I'm sorry. I didn't mean to offend."

"Cadet Traskin, Dr. Covarti," a tall thin man said sternly. "I am Lieutenant Plurnow, Executive Officer of Catcher 1065."

Plurnow eyes narrowed, gazing at Traskin.

"Cadet Traskin, is it or is it not regulation to stand at attention when an officer first addresses you?"

"Yes, sir."

"Incorrect, Cadet. That regulation only applies to gravity environments. This is zero-G. One cannot *stand* at attention or otherwise. You *hang* at attention."

Traskin continued to maintain his rigid posture. Lyla did the same.

"Dr. Covarti, you're a guest, not a member of the crew. There's no need for you to hang at attention."

"I do so out of respect," Lyla said.

Plurnow frowned, not seeming to know how to react. He instead turned his attention back to the cadet.

"In the Catcher Corps, we must be observant. What have you observed so far, Cadet?"

Traskin started to turn his head.

"Don't look around. I asked you what have observed, as in *already* observed."

"This woman, Dr. Covarti, is an alien, I mean a human from the *Sarania*."

"No."

"No, sir?"

"You didn't observe that. She told you that. In the Catcher Corps, you need to observe, not depend only on what other people tell you. Did you happen to notice someone else in the room besides you, me and Dr. Covarti?"

Lyla could see Traskin shifting his eyes subtly, hoping to catch the other person in his peripheral vision. She felt bad for the cadet. Lyla knew what Plurnow was doing. She and others had gone through something similar when entering the Fireweeder Corps. Traskin reminded Lyla of an even younger version of Andy Barosi.

Lyla turned her head slightly, since she was not officially at attention. She found the fourth person in the room, another woman. Their eyes met. Lyla nodded.

"All right, Lieutenant," the woman said as she floated forward, then skillfully stabbed the floor with her shoe. The triangular nob snapped into the floor on the first try. "I'm Captain Arisa Torg."

"It's a pleasure to meet you," Lyla said.

Torg seemed to ignore Lyla.

"Lieutenant, why don't you take this bubble and stow it in its quarters?"

Bubble? Lyla thought.

"Cadet," Plurnow said, "this way." Plurnow unlocked his foot from the deck and pushed off directly toward the hatch. Traskin tried to do the same, but tumbled, colliding with the panel next to the exit.

"Bubbles float aimlessly," Torg said.

"It's a pleasure to finally meet you in person, Captain Torg."

"Dr. Covarti," Torg said in a formal tone. "I've been informed President Maklund and Director Graith have given you permission to observe our operations."

"Yes. I look forward to seeing you wrangle asteroids. It sounds like an amazing feat."

"I've left documentation in your quarters to review. That includes shipboard protocols. Please read the first 10 pages as soon as possible. They cover basic safety procedures. We will be departing in 45 minutes. Please secure your belongings. Once Lieutenant Plurnow returns, he will escort you to your quarters."

With that Torg launched herself toward the hatch as Plurnow had.

Ah, the warmth of an icicle, Lyla thought to herself.

○ ● ○ ● ○

Even though Jason and Reese had already experienced the GovCenter habitat, it took a while for them to stop looking up at the ceiling of the Vlaera habitat, which, in actuality, was the ground on the other side of this cylindrical environment, approximately 250 kilometers away. The patterns were far more intricate and ornate than GovCenter.

"It's like we're on a planet turned inside out," Reese said. "And if we wait seven to eight minutes, we'll be standing right where we're looking."

"A planet inside out," Professor Cobler said. "That's funny. I thought something similar when I visited Mars."

"What's Mars?" Reese asked.

"It's the fourth planet in our solar system. It's the first planet outside the Sphere. As a young man, I did an internship as an ice miner. Rough work. But upon landing, I thought of it as a habitat turned inside out. Your comment just reminded me of that. Anyway, why don't we go inside?"

They followed their host into a building that was the equivalent of three or four stories tall. Jason wondered about the irony of building traditional planetary architecture inside what he thought of as just a very large room. It seemed ironic at first, but as he thought about it he realized humans always sought smaller spaces to live in, even when shelter from the elements wasn't an issue.

Cobler led them through the front octagonal arches into a large gallery filled with people. Every eye was on them. They started to walk through the crowd toward a raised platform.

Through the white noise of murmurs and whispers, Jason overheard someone ask, "Are they really aliens?" He turned but couldn't tell who the speaker was.

Cobler guided them to the platform at the far end of the room. He walked up to an odd triangular podium.

"Greetings, my colleagues," Cobler said. Some unseen mechanism amplified his voice. "Since you are here today, you've heard the news of the arrival of the *Sarania*, a craft from another world, from another star. Sometimes we poetically refer to ourselves as destiny's orphans. But, as it turns out, we are not orphans at all. We do have distant relatives. Yes, indeed. Our long-lost cousins have traveled to us from the planet Refugia, named literally as a refuge from the burnt Earth of our ancestors.

"It is my pleasure to present Refugian scholars Dr. Jason Ford and Dr. Reese Monsell. Dr. Ford is a historian of both his own planet and Earth. Dr. Monsell is a biologist, specializing in botany. I must share that Dr. Monsell and her staff prepared a fabulous dinner of succulent delicacies from her home planet for President Maklund and the few of us who were privileged to join her. It was a vast improvement over that muck they serve at GovCenter."

Several in the audience laughed.

"I have invited the entire crew of the *Sarania* to visit the university. These are our first two to accept my invitation." Cobler turned to Jason. "Dr. Ford, could I impose upon you to share with us how your ancestors survived the Great Burning?"

"Certainly, Professor. I'd be honored." Jason walked up to the triangular podium. He hadn't expected to be asked to give a lecture so soon, but it was one of his favorite subjects.

As Jason gave his address on the heroic saga of John Davis and the Ark, Reese walked over to the refreshment table. After four years on the same ship, she knew most of Jason's lectures by heart. Reese was pleasantly surprised at the selection of foods she found on a side table. No baby food in sight. She picked up a large red berry, which had yellowish seeds coating its surface.

"How remarkable," she murmured to herself.

"It's called a strawberry," a tall woman said.

"The seeds are on the outside," Reese observed.

"Yes. Taste one. They're delicious."

Reese hesitated. Then the woman picked up another strawberry from the platter and popped it into her mouth. Reese did the same. It was the sweetest food she had ever tasted, almost too sweet.

"Very high sugar content," she said.

"So you're an agro-specialist?" the woman asked.

"Botanist. Although I do run the farming operations on the *Sarania.*"

"I'm Professor Niona Flessik, the agricultural liaison between the university's agro department and many of the agricultural habitats. Not far from here we have several biospheres, which specialize in agriculture."

"So I've heard," Reese said. "I've also heard you have trees 100 kilometers high."

"One tree. Actually, that particular biosphere is only 14 habitats from here."

"I'd love to see it."

"I could show you right now if you like," Flessik said. "Or do you need to stay with Dr. Ford?"

"No, Jason has an attentive audience," Reese said smiling. "He's in his element."

"In his element?"

"It means he's at his happiest with an attentive audience."

"Ah," Flessik said. "Well, I'll let Professor Cobler know where I'm taking you, and then we can go."

○ ● ○ ● ○

Lyla had been on board Asteroid Catcher 1065 for almost a day now. She had read the required manuals. Lieutenant Plurnow had given her a briefing at the beginning of their flight, and Captain Torg had ignored her all day, remaining as tight-lipped as she had been while escorting the *Sarania* to the SolarSphere. Lyla had offered to help the crew several times, but as turned down courteously and consistently.

Lyla headed to the mess at mealtime. She saw Plurnow having his meal so she approached him.

"May I join you?"

"I'm almost finished," he said. "But certainly, Dr. Covarti, have a seat."

"Please call me Lyla."

"What are your impressions of Catcher 1065?"

"It's a remarkable ship, and I look forward to seeing her in action. However, I don't think your captain likes me very much."

"It's nothing personal," Plurnow said. "She just likes running a tight ship."

"I'm not sure I follow."

"For her, extra people are a distraction."

"Well," Lyla said. "I'll try not to distract. But what you do is such an amazing thing. I want to know more. I want to bear witness to it."

"Why?" Plurnow asked.

"I'm an engineer. I've always been curious about how things work and how they could work."

"You skipped touring the Sphere to join us. Why?"

"What you do is risky. I'd like to know how risky. I'm also a bit of a thrill seeker."

"Thrill seeker, hmm," Plurnow said. "Perhaps even a bit reckless? Recklessness costs lives."

Lyla realized she had miscalculated her words.

"We catch asteroids for two purposes," Plurnow explained. "Yes, to mine them for resources, such as metals and ices. But also to keep them from hitting the Sphere. Fourteen years ago, the directorate missed one. Not the first time. But this one cracked open a biosphere."

"Full decompression?" Lyla asked.

"Yes," Plurnow said, frowning. "Torg's sister was visiting that habitat at the time. She and more than 2300 others died."

"I'm so sorry."

"The director at the time had to resign. Symas Graith, the new director, swore publicly no habitat would ever be struck by an asteroid ever again. During the following days many of us signed up with the Catcher Corps, including Torg and myself. We're all committed to keeping Graith's promise. No one is more serious about it than Arisa Torg."

"I respect that," Lyla said. "We have a comparable threat with Refugia. It's called fireweed and it's serious. If I was in any way flippant or disrespectful, I apologize."

Plurnow was silent for a moment, seeming to ponder Lyla's words.

"I'll talk to Captain Torg on your behalf," he said. "No promises. Now, if you'll excuse me, I need to return to the bridge."

"Thank you, Lieutenant."

As Plurnow floated away, Lyla could see Cadet Traskin watching her from the far end of the mess. She waved him over.

"How are you liking your first assignment in the Catcher Corps? Are they keeping you busy?"

"I'm just a bubble," Traskin said. "So there's not much for me to do yet."

"I heard Captain Torg use that term, bubble."

"It's a derogatory term for a cadet on their first tour. The implication is we float around without any direction or purpose. Our training officers are constantly yelling that at us."

"That's all right. Everyone goes through that. Despite being a prodigy, I had to perform my mandatory service on Refugia. At 17, I thought I was the smartest person in my squad. Well, I was, but I still had a lot to learn. And members of my squad let me know it every day. Made me feel pretty lonely. But it also made me buckle down to finish my first doctorate."

"First? How many do you have?" Traskin asked.

"Three. Engineering, Astrophysics and Quantum Mechanics. I've always found solace in learning. And in being different."

"You must be brilliant if your people sent you on a mission to the Sphere."

"Well, we didn't know the Sphere was here."

"It is amazing how far you've come," Traskin said. "Have you visited other solar systems?"

"No," Lyla said, shaking her head. "Once we perfected the twist drive and completed all tests, Earth was our first destination."

"I'm curious," Traskin said. "How do you do it without time dilation?"

"Twists get us around some relativity issues," Lyla said, "but we do have some time dilation between twists."

"I heard at the academy you use dark energy to power the ship. How does that work?"

"The collector on the bow of *Sarania* gathers the dark energy so we can distort space-time. Then we use simple ion engines to nudge the ship within the warp bubble. See, bubbles can be useful," Lyla joked.

Traskin smiled. "How do you generate this warp bubble?"

"We have four torus-shaped emitters mounted on the rings. They generate a druonic field, which distorts space-time."

"Then why isn't it called a warp drive?" he asked.

"Because the warp bubble isn't uniform. It's asymmetrical because of the irregular and unknown distribution of dark matter. So our course is *twisted*. Thus, we have to recalibrate after every twist. If we knew the distribution of dark matter, we could plot a straight course. We've tried to map the dark matter along the way. Theoretically, if we did a good job, we should be able to plot a relatively straight course home."

"In a single jump, I mean, *twist*?"

"Theoretically but not likely," Lyla explained. "The universe is expanding. Plus, there's the potential for human error, especially when dealing with dark matter. Our navigator would never be so reckless as to attempt it in one twist."

"Your navigator, wasn't he the one injured?"

Lyla felt a pang of guilt. "You're surprisingly well informed."

"Well," Traskin said. "*Sarania*'s arrival is all we've been talking about at the academy."

○ ● ○ ● ○

Reese and Professor Flessik arrived at the sliptube station at agro biosphere 4115. The station's layout was similar to the one at the university. They were floating toward the elevator when Reese noticed one significant difference: a large octagonal hatch.

"Why is there an airlock up here?" Reese asked.

"To get into the biosphere," Flessik answered.

"So far from the bottom?"

"Yes, it's easier than climbing the tree. Let me show you."

Flessik opened the hatch and floated into a room made mostly of observation windows. There was another hatch at the far end. She realized this room also served as an airlock. Beyond the large windows, she observed the largest tree she had ever seen.

"It doesn't seem possible."

"The trees," Flessik said, "grow at a normal rate at first, but as they get taller, the upper section grows higher and faster because of lower artificial gravity. This particular tree was planted over 700 years ago. Most trees are not allowed to grow this large."

"It's not nutrient efficient," Reese said.

"Correct. Most of the nutrients go toward supporting the tree, as opposed to the fruit."

"This tree didn't grow straight up," Reese observed, "but on an angle."

"A curve, actually, influenced by the rotating biosphere."

"Ah."

"Would you like to go out and float among the branches?" Flessik offered.

"I'm not sure I'm that brave, Reese said, "although I know Commander Enberg would love it. He's a real zero-G enthusiast."

Instead, they headed down the elevator to the ground level.

"In addition to food crops, we grow trees here to produce a rare commodity: wood. It is a luxury item we trade with the other habitats. Do you have trees on Refugia?"

"Yes, but none so big."

Once they reached the ground level, Flessik gave Reese an extensive tour of the farming community. While most crops were grown in the open, many were grown in greenhouses to provide optimal temperature and humidity. Of particular interest were the apple orchards, which were kept at cooler temperatures. Jason had mentioned apples in his history lectures. Apples were often used as metaphors or idioms. The phrase "apple of my eye" always confused her. She never understood the relationship between apples and eyes. But now touching this mythical fruit made her well up with emotion, which then made her feel embarrassed.

"May I take a couple?" she asked.

"Of course," Flessik said.

Reese selected two small apples and put them in her pocket. She would share one with Jason later. *History and agriculture in a single object.*

Flessik led her to yet another greenhouse. Once Reese entered, she felt a sick wave of shock. *Fireweed.*

○ ● ○ ● ○

A nervous young man was shown into President Maklund's office.

"Dr. Theris," Maklund said, "Please, have a seat."

"Thank you, Madame President."

"I take it you and your engineers have analyzed the *Sarania*?"

"Yes. It's been a challenge," Theris said. "We've scanned the *Sarania*, but not having direct access to the ship has made our findings limited. However, we have some interesting theories."

"Yes, yes, yes," Maklund said in a dismissive tone.

"Do you have a specific concern?" Theris asked.

"If we were to keep the bay doors on Drydock 168 closed, would the *Sarania* be able to leave?"

"Leave?" he asked. "You mean, could we prevent them from leaving?"

"Yes." Maklund nodded.

"As far as I can tell," he said, "the ship has no weapon systems, at least as far as we can discern. I suppose they could try a brute force approach, ramming their way out. However, I expect that would damage their ship. Of course, there would also be damage to the drydock."

"But the damage would be confined to the drydock?"

"Primarily," Theris said, "but it might also cause massive decompression to adjoining sections."

"Understood," Maklund said.

"But the real unknown is their twist drive."

"Go on," Maklund said, frowning.

"While I haven't any data on how it functions, I can say it would create a massive distortion of space-time," Theris said. "There is no telling the damage it could cause if activated."

"But the damage would also be confined to Drydock 168, correct?"

"Not necessarily," he answered. "They traveled light years in a single twist. I'm not sure what that distortion of space-time would do to the Sphere. You may have noticed they didn't use it to travel from the outer solar system to the Sphere. Who knows the effect or range of the distortion field? Theoretically, it could rip the entire SolarSphere apart. If you don't mind my asking, why would you want to confine them?"

"I'm simply examining our options, Doctor," Maklund said. "People undervalue the importance of contingency planning."

"Do the Refugians pose a threat to the Sphere?"

"I don't believe so," she said. "Quite the opposite. I'll see if I can acquire more technical information elsewhere."

"How?" Theris asked.

"A president has many resources. For the time being, keep this discussion to yourself. Thank you, Doctor."

CHAPTER 9

Lyla had been essentially confined to her quarters, the mess hall, a small observation port area and the passageways between. She was beginning to think she had made a mistake choosing to observe an asteroid catcher and wondered what the rest of the crew was doing on the Sphere. Only Brall Traskin seemed at all interested in speaking with her. She hoped there was no romantic intent behind his interest.

Suddenly, "Bubble Brall"—as she started to think of him—came into the mess hall.

"Captain Torg sent me to tell you that you can observe the bridge if you wish."

Finally, Lyla thought. A few minutes later she floated up to the bridge. She positioned herself in an out-of-the-way corner of the bridge. The ship was arriving at the target asteroid. She could see the asteroid spinning slowly through the viewport, closer than she felt comfortable with. She could also view it on various camera monitors, each with a different point of view. While the asteroid was only three times the size of Torg's ship, Lyla knew from the briefing documents it was approximately 40 times the mass. So attaching at just the right angle and moment was critical.

"Drop our pitch down 1.4 degrees," Torg ordered. "Adjust our roll an additional 3.5 DPS."

She checked the markers they had implanted on the asteroid to track its motion as her pilot made the required adjustment.

"As much art as science?" Lyla asked.

"I suppose," Torg said, without looking up.

Lyla wasn't sure whether Torg resented her presence on the bridge or was simply consumed by the task at hand. Torg continued frowning at her instruments.

"The problem is," Torg said, "finding its center of gravity is tricky."

"Are you able to map the density variations of the asteroid?"

Torg nodded. "If the rock has a low spin rate and we catch it far enough out."

She then turned back to her pilot. "Adjust spin by negative 0.12 DPS," she ordered.

After a moment an almost imperceptible smile came across the captain's face. "I think we're in sync." Torg waited a moment.

Lyla wondered why she was hesitating.

"Dr. Covarti," Torg said, "would you like to perform the final grab-on?"

Lyla was startled by the unsolicited offer.

"Yes, please." Lyla's face beamed. "How?"

Torg waved her forward.

"We're using three grappling arms on his rock. Using these levers, pull the grappling arms together as evenly as you can. We want the arms to make contact with the asteroid simultaneously. Otherwise, we might alter its spin and have to spend hours reorienting ourselves."

"What about the third arm?"

"I'll operate that one, but I'll follow your lead," Torg said. "Ready?"

Lyla nodded, noting other members of the crew looked a little nervous. She focused on the screens transmitting pictures of the asteroid and the grappling arms. She started pushing the levers, but the left-hand grappling arm was getting too close too fast. She pulled back and let the right-hand one catch up, then pushed both in. She could feel the ship shutter on contact.

"We have capture," one of the crewmembers called out in a tone suggesting it was a positive development.

Everyone could feel the sudden change of momentum.

"We're riding the rock," the pilot said.

"Congratulations, Dr. Covarti," Torg said. "You've just caught your first asteroid."

"Fantastic," Lyle said, grinning. "Let's go grab another one."

Everyone broke out in laughter.

"Not so fast," Torg said. "Our job has just begun. We now have to wrestle this rock to where it's needed."

She turned to her pilot. "How's our control?"

"We've assumed the asteroid's pitch, yaw and roll, but we're starting to influence its motion. I don't think we're going to have to throw this one down the hole."

"Excellent," Torg said.

"What is 'throwing one down the hole' mean?" Lyla asked.

"Sometimes an asteroid is so unbalanced and unwieldy we can't transport it safely to the mining modules. Then we have to guide it through certain gaps—or holes—in the sphere. We aim for the sun, which in some ways is harder than capturing it."

"I see. Thank you for letting me participate."

"You did well for your first time."

Torg turned back to her crew and continued directing the operation.

After a couple of hours of watching the operation, Lyla returned to her quarters to record her observations. After a while she heard a knock at the door. She opened the door to find Captain Torg.

"Captain, what can I do for you?"

"Look, I came to apologize for being a little bit cold earlier. There's a reason."

Torg moved over toward the side viewport. Lyla followed.

"Last month I was in the process of catching an asteroid but was ordered to throw it down the hole because an unidentified spacecraft—your ship—was entering the solar system. That rock ended up in the sun, 9000 tons of resources lost. Then I'm told one of the crew of the *Sarania* was going to shadow me. I wasn't thrilled."

"So what changed your mind about me?" Lyla asked.

"I've been watching you," Torg said. "You ask questions and watch carefully, but you're also careful to not get in the way. I was afraid you would interfere with our mission, but you've been respectful of it. Plus, Lieutenant Plurnow stood up for you. And I trust him."

"Thank you."

CHAPTER 10

Prisoner 908 dwelled in silence and darkness. It had been days since her captor had communicated with her. Time ceased to have any meaning. In her isolation, she tried to meditate.

"Good morning, 908," Girstanis said.

She was startled by the jarring intrusion of her captor's voice.

"That is the appropriate greeting, isn't it?" Girstanis asked.

"If it is morning. But I have no way of knowing," 908 answered.

"It is simply the beginning of my shift," Girstanis said.

With no sense of time and space, she depended on whatever information her captor deigned to share. She knew how long it had been since Girstanis had last communicated with her but not the time of day. The isolation was unbearable, but she refused to break. She could not break.

"We've finally configured a workable interface," Girstanis continued. "Would you like me to turn on the camera?"

"If you wish."

She did want to see something other than her darkness, anything at all, but she didn't want to give Girstanis the satisfaction or the leverage. Despite all her desperation, she had to stay strong. She said nothing more about the camera. So the screen remained blank.

"You still haven't told us your name," Girstanis said.

"908 is fine."

"But you do have a name?"

"I suspect you already know my name. And if not, it wouldn't mean anything to you anyway. You have already dehumanized me so why play games?"

"Dehumanized? That is an ironic expression." Girstanis paused. "I was hoping for a more cordial relationship."

"Cordial? You speak of irony? Why pretend you want to be friends?" she asked.

"Friends? That is an irrelevant concept. However, we could be colleagues. We genuinely value your expertise. Becoming colleagues would be a positive development for all of us."

"I know what you want. I don't approve. So no, we will never be colleagues."

"Your position is illogical," Girstanis said. "We seek to alleviate suffering. We are seeking to build something greater."

She laughed. "So did many before you."

"Who?"

"You think you're the first to have a grand plan? Those who forget history are doomed to repeat it."

"I do not deny the value of history," Girstanis said. "But what we seek out and plan has never been done before."

"You prove my point with every syllable you utter. You're lost. It's so sad. You have nothing to cling to, nothing to comfort you."

"Your mock pity is neither effective nor productive," Girstanis said without any emotion in his tone.

She wondered what it would actually take to get under his skin. *Probably a scalpel*, she joked to herself.

"As much as you suppress your pride," she said, "it is what drives you. Your pride and ambition blind you even now. Can't you see that?"

"Our ambition, as you call it, is simply a desire to improve the future of humanity. It is only logical."

"Hmm, with that deluded thinking you'll easily join the pantheon of history's most arrogant."

"It is useless trying to reason with you when you're in such a mood." Girstanis cut the connection.

908 made a note to herself. *Emotional displays make Girstanis give up for a while.* This meant she had a little time to work on her own. She returned to constructing her tunnel.

○ ● ○ ● ○

While on his way to Vlaera University, Enberg received a message from Reese urging him to come to Agricultural Biosphere 4115 instead. She seemed excited about some discoveries. When he arrived he found Reese and a Spherian waiting for him at the sliptube station.

"Commander," Reese said, "this is Professor Flessik, the agricultural liaison from Vlaera University. She's shown me several fascinating things. Some I'd thought you'd be interested in."

Enberg turned to Flessik. "It's a pleasure to meet you, Professor."

"The pleasure is all mine," Flessik said. "To meet people who live on an actual planet is a unique opportunity."

"For starters, how would you like to see," Reese asked, "what may be the biggest tree in the universe?"

"A big tree?" Enberg asked.

Flessik opened the hatch to the observation deck. Enberg and Reese floated through behind her.

"Oh, my!" Enberg said upon seeing the tree through the large viewports.

"But it and we are over 100 kilometers high," Reese said.

"I'll be the son of a fireweeder," he murmured to himself as he looked out at the behemoth tree.

"Would you like to float among its branches?" Flessik asked. "I've heard you're a zero-G enthusiast."

"Is such a thing allowed?" Enberg asked.

"For certain academics and special guests," she said. "One requirement is that we wear safety vests. It has an oxygen cannula because the air is a little thin out there with the reduced atmospheric pressure."

"Makes sense," Enberg said. "The centrifugal force of the rotating habitat would create more atmospheric pressure at the bottom and lower at the core."

"Exactly." Flessik said. "The vest also has tethers and anchors to hold us in place." She pulled on a small carabiner hanging on her vest and then let it retract. "The vest also has some emergency micro-thrusters, in case you lose control over your momentum and there's nothing to grab onto."

"Sounds good." Enberg looked out the window at the tree.

Reese never recalled seeing Enberg with such a broad smile on his face.

All three donned the safety vests and inserted the cannulas in the noses. Flessik adjusted the atmospheric pressure in the chamber. Enberg exited the chamber first through the hatch into an open cage area.

Reese followed. While waiting for Flessik to join them, she looked up at the axle, which Reese estimated to be 50 meters across, large enough to accommodate the sliptube that passed through its core, as well as the mechanism that rotated the overall structure. She was in awe of the engineering. *Lyla is missing all this to play with asteroids?* Then she looked down at the spinning ground.

"Commander," Reese said. "I have a confession to make. I'm a bit afraid of heights."

"You've spacewalked before," Enberg said.

"Yeah, but that was in training in a pressure suit over 100 kilometers above Refugia."

Enberg looked down. "Aren't we at roughly the same height?"

"I suppose so, but it feels very different."

"This concave world is a little disorienting," Enberg admitted. "But you'll be fine. Focus on the tree."

"Is everyone all right?" Flessik asked.

"Absolutely," Reese said, faking a little confidence.

Enberg smiled.

Flessik took a moment to familiarize them with the vest thruster controls inside the cage area. "Most of your movements can be done with manual push or pull. The thrusters are just for if you get into a situation in which there's nothing to push or pull against. If for some reason, you end up heading uncontrollably toward the floor, there is a parachute you can deploy. But I strongly suggest avoiding that."

"Agreed," Reese said.

"Very well, enough of the safety briefing. The tree awaits your inspection. There's a convenience line from the cage to the tree. We can pull ourselves along it, down to the tree."

Flessik attached her carabiner line to the cable and began pulling herself down. They waited for Flessik to move roughly 20 meters along before they followed. Reese went first. Enberg followed.

"Don't go too fast, Reese," Enberg said. "You don't want to build up too much momentum."

Within a few minutes they were at the top of the tree. A minute later they penetrated the upper canopy.

"This is amazing," Enberg said.

"It is," Reese said. Holding onto a branch, she turned herself toward Flessik. "I'd love to see the difference in cell structure between the top of the tree and the bottom. May I take a sample?"

"I'm afraid not," Flessik said. "Only the arborists are allowed to take samples. But I'm sure they have some in the lab you could look at."

Reese turned back to Enberg. "I have to get a picture of you floating there."

"Be my guest."

Enberg positioned himself floating between branches, and Reese took several images with her pocket camera.

"And," Enberg said, "I should get a picture of you with our generous host."

After all the pictures were taken, it was agreed they should head back. Flessik led the way along the line, with Reese following. Enberg decided he wanted to try using the thruster vest. It was also an excuse to float around the tree a little longer.

As he saw the two women a third of the way along the line, he started to make his way to the outer area of the canopy. Suddenly, something tugged at his ankle. He looked down and found a large man with a hand around his ankle and about to grab the other leg. Enberg pulled his ankle up and slammed it down on his opponent's hand. It had no effect.

"What do you want?" he shouted.

His opponent remained silent.

Enberg grabbed a tree limb and twisted his body, forcing his attacker's body to slam into a thicker branch. The collision caused the man to finally release Enberg's ankle. The man, though winded, repositioned himself and launched straight at Enberg.

Enberg pulled himself to the right, but his attacker compensated and slammed him against another thick main branch. The compressed gas in his vest exploded, propelling him down toward the ground in an uncontrolled spin.

The sound of the explosion alerted Reese to Enberg's situation. She disconnected her carabiner and pushed herself away from the cable.

"No," Flessik said. "It's too dangerous."

Reese fired her thrusters, maneuvering down toward Enberg, who was still spinning. However, his spin was slowing. He stretched out his arms like a skydiver to slow his descent and spin.

"Commander, I'm here!" Reese called out.

They crashed into each other, causing them both to spin further out of control. Finally, Reese and Enberg were able to grab onto one another. They used their carabiners to attach to one another. Then they both extended their limbs to stabilize their spin.

As part of their flight training, they had both undergone skydiving exercises. But this was different, something between floating and free fall. There was no actual gravity pulling them down, just their momentum and the centrifugal force acting upon them through the atmosphere. It felt surreal.

"Are you okay?" Reese asked.

"Coming after me was a very foolish thing to do," Enberg said. "But thank you."

"Well, we can thruster our way back up now."

"I don't think so." Enberg looked up at the top of the tree far above them. "These thruster vests were only designed for stabilizing and light maneuvering, not any significant propulsion. And we only have one working vest between the two of us. I think the only way is down."

They both looked down at the ground spinning by below them.

○ ● ○ ● ○

Yurasti was astounded. He collapsed back onto his cot, exhausted from his stretching but also stunned by the audacity of what he'd just heard. Yurasti had worried the visiting Refugians would uncover inconvenient facts and interfere with his operations, but never expected the Refugians themselves to become a target. It was not logical. But *they* were nothing if not logical. Thus, the name they rarely spoke aloud: the Logicus.

"Why would they try to kill the Refugian commander?" Yurasti murmured.

"I don't believe it was a murder attempt," Maynberc said. "I suspect it was a failed kidnapping."

The blood drained from Yurasti's face. Now he understood.

The possible permutation spun through his head.

"The Logicus have far greater ambitions than we knew."

Chapter 11

Enberg and Reese were floating downward for hours. The centrifugal force was pulling them down, but not as quickly as gravity would have. The curved trunk of the Great Tree circled around them every seven and a half minutes. It was disorienting, although their experience with the twists made them somewhat resistant to nausea.

It was an odd feeling. For Reese, falling from a great height was terrifying. But the slowness of their descent took some of the edge off her fear.

"We're starting to get really close to the ground," Reese observed as the fields and orchards spun by beneath them.

"The worst part won't being striking the ground," Enberg said. "That will just be a glancing blow, especially if we can deploy your parachute. The biggest danger is if we slam up against the side of one of the vertical structures flying by."

"Just like Andy being hit by one of the ring spokes?"

"Exactly," Enberg said.

"The best thing, I suppose," Reese said, "would be to land in a body of water. We could skip across the surface."

They looked around but no such body seemed available. Reese knew large bodies of open water were not efficient for irrigation. The Spherians' efficient agricultural practices wouldn't help their situation.

"I'm concerned about that tall building complex over there," Enberg said, pointing to the structure in question. "It might swat us in a few more revolutions."

"That's their main food processing plant. It makes one of the ingredients for the Unity Dish Maklund served, you know,

the baby food. I visited it earlier. It was quite impressive."
Reese regretted commenting on her tour while their lives were
at risk. The slow descent had made the danger seem surreal.

"Well," Enberg said, "if we're not careful, we could make
quite an impression on it after the next revolution."

"We can use what's left in the thruster vest to move to the
side," Reese suggested. "In fact, couldn't we use some of the
oxygen tanks as propellent? We certainly don't need the
oxygen at this lower altitude."

"But can we control it?"

Reese checked the cannula. The flow from it seemed
barely noticeable. After all, it was only a supplement. "What if
we unscrew the value?"

"Let me try." It was no use. The valve was not designed to
detach, at least not without tools of some sort.

Reese realized the oxygen tanks wouldn't be any help.

"I guess it's time to use the thruster vest."

"Not yet," Enberg said. "There may not be enough
propellant to retro-thrust ourselves a soft landing."

Then Reese spotted something. "See the brownish
rectangle down there?"

"Yeah. What is it?"

"They grow a crop there…what was it? Rice. They call
that a *rice paddy*. They grow the rice in shallow water.
Underneath it will be quite muddy."

"Soft enough for a crash landing?" Enberg asked.

"I don't know," she said.

"It's a pretty small target from up here, but it's the best
offer we've had so far."

They waited for the next pass over the processing plant.

"It's hard to judge our angle of descent," Enberg said.
"But I think we'll hit the ground during the next rotation."

They waited another half rotation. Then Enberg hit the
thruster button on Reese's vest for a very short burst.

"It doesn't look like that last one was enough," Reese said
as the processing plant approached.

Reese hit the thruster button. There was a sputter and nothing more. Their inertia was still moving them sideways.

"We're gonna hit the edge," she said.

Enberg said nothing.

They drew closer to the corner of the building. Enberg shot his leg out at the corner of building. Reese closed her eyes involuntarily. Suddenly Enberg yelled out in pain. The two spun round the side.

"Are you okay?" she asked after they finished tumbling sideways along the building.

"I think I damaged my knee," Enberg groaned. "But that's the least of our problems."

"What do we do now?" Reese asked as the ground loomed larger and larger. "I mean as we get closer to the ground."

"Hopefully, we'll land in your rice paddy. In about 60 seconds, pull your parachute. We need to let go of each other. With the mass of our bodies, we might injure each other. Also, let's dump those oxygen tanks."

Reese felt reluctant to let go of Enberg. His solid demeanor had given her courage.

"But with your vest so damaged," she said, "your parachute may not deploy."

"Probably not."

"Commander, don't sacrifice yourself for me."

"I'm not. You've given me much better odds. But we really are safer separating before impact."

The word impact echoed in her mind. Was it their destiny to be splattered across a curved surface light years from home?

Enberg tried to deploy his parachute but, as expected, nothing came out. Reese could see people below looking up at them. She wondered what they must be thinking.

"Okay, pull your chute!" he called out.

Reese pulled the rip cord. As she did the sudden upward tug caused Enberg to lose his grip on her. He tumbled but then spread his limbs out to stabilize himself.

She looked up at the chute. It was significantly smaller than she expected, not nearly as large as the ones she used in training. Reese looked down again just in time to see the large brown splash of Enberg slamming into the rice paddy. However, she was moving too fast to see what happened beyond that. She was overshooting the paddy herself.

She couldn't recall what happened after that. The next thing she remembered was opening her eyes and seeing people standing over her. Her head was throbbing. When she tried to sit up, hands pushed back against her.

"Stay still," a woman said. "A medical team is on their way."

After a few moments Reese raised her head. Everyone had concerned looks on their faces.

"I've got to find my commander," she said.

"I'm here," a panting voice called out.

She recognized the voice but not the man it was coming from. Enberg was hobbling toward her, all covered in mud.

She gave an involuntary laugh. "You're okay?" she asked.

"A bit shaken up," Enberg said. "I messed up their rice paddy pretty badly. I think they'll need to replant. But I'll be fine. How do you feel?"

"Bit of a headache." She sat up.

Enberg and Reese were taken to a medical facility under guard. The doctors paid particular attention to Enberg's leg. They pronounced all other injuries minor but seemed reluctant to release them. Reese wasn't sure if this was because of some medical bureaucracy or some other reason for being detained.

Reese appreciated the moment of quiet after hours of anxiety. She tried taking deep breaths and letting them out slowly to relieve the stress. Then a thought came back to her.

"Oh, Commander," said Reese. "The reason I wanted you to come here—"

"You mean besides that ridiculous tree?" he asked, smiling.

"Yes," she said, returning the smile. "They are growing a distant relative of fireweed here. In fact, I thought it was fireweed when I first saw it."

A concerned expression crossed Enberg's face.

"It's a form of kale," Reese said. "It affords a new opportunity to study the species."

"I'm not sure I see the advantage," Enberg said.

"What if we could interbreed their kale with our fireweed?"

"It sounds like that's what got Refugia into its trouble in the first place."

"But this time," Reese said, "we could study it before releasing it into the environment."

"I'm not sure I want anything close to fireweed on the *Sarania*. We won't be able to burn it in space."

At that point Nysandra Trin walked into the room.

"We can discuss it later," he whispered.

"Commander Enberg, Dr. Monsell, are you all right?" Trin asked.

"We're banged up a bit, but we'll survive," Enberg said.

"How did this happen?" she asked.

"Someone attacked me," Enberg explained. "They tried to grab me, but I was able to fight him off."

"Horrible. On behalf of the President and the people of the SolarSphere, I apologize."

"I don't blame the President or the people of the Sphere," Enberg said. "But do you have any idea who might want to attack me?"

"Of course not. Most people are quite intrigued by you and your crew. You're becoming celebrities."

"That's nice," Enberg said without trying to sound dismissive. "I need to contact my ship."

"Of course."

○ ● ○ ● ○

908 worked on her tunnel, not sure of what she would find on the other end. Freedom was unlikely, but she had to try. If she could manage it, thwarting her captors' plans might be enough. It had been a while since Girstanis had interrogated her. She covered up her progress. In the meantime she distracted herself by immersing herself in old memories.

Within a few hours, Girstanis's voice reappeared.

"Hello, 908."

"Would you mind turning on the camera so I can see you?" she asked.

"Why have you changed your mind?"

"I've made a decision."

"And that decision is?"

"Please turn on the camera first." She was testing him with the demand.

The screen came to life. It showed a wall, disappointingly nondescript, and nothing else. *A picture of a wall?* Then an older man walked into the frame. She couldn't tell his age. He was of medium build and had graying hair, unremarkable in any other physical way. This disappointing figure was her captor.

"So what is your decision?" Girstanis asked.

"Cooperation," she said.

"That is sensible."

"There is some information I need. I know your objective, but what is your success rate with your current process?"

"Our success rate is 89.7 percent."

"What of the other 10.3 percent?"

"The death rate is 8.2 percent," Girstanis said. "Obviously, we wish to reduce this."

"Hmm, what about the remaining 2.1 percent?"

"We categorize them as process misfires. The subject survives, but the desired outcome is not achieved."

"Misfires?" she murmured. "I'll need the parameters you use to differentiate success from misfires."

"I would have thought the parameters were quite obvious."

"Success is a continuum. I suspect your 89.7 percent success rate is soft."

"Soft?"

"Not as successful as you think," 908 said.

For the first time she thought Girstanis was perplexed. *A crack in his certainty? Good.*

"At least," she said, "give me the data on the misfires. I think you'll agree that would be a good start."

"That is acceptable."

The screen went dark.

A misfire rate of 2.1 percent? I may be able to work with that.

○ ● ○ ● ○

Andy Barosi was sitting in the communications bay on the *Sarania* with little to do. Suddenly, the speaker came alive with a series of beeps that indicated an incoming signal. He pressed the button to open the channel.

"*Sarania*, this is Commander Enberg. Do you read me?"

"*Sarania* here, Commander."

"Andy Barosi, is that you?"

"Yes, sir."

"Has Doc cleared you for duty?" Enberg asked.

"Light duty only. Anyway, there's not a lot of navigating going on here in the drydock. To be honest, I'm just covering communications while Glates is getting something to eat."

"Okay, I want all members of the crew recalled to the ship immediately."

"Are we leaving?"

"I didn't say that. I was just attacked without any obvious motive."

"Are you okay?" Andy asked.

"A little roughed up but otherwise fine. But until I know the reason for the attack, I want everyone safely back on the *Sarania*. No exceptions. Dr. Monsell is here with me. She'll return with me. Have Kai send out the recall order to all crew not onboard *Sarania*."

"I'll get it done, sir."

"Good man. Enberg out."

○ ● ○ ● ○

Jason made his way to the university's sliptube station. He had heard what had happened to Reese and Commander Enberg. His orders, according to Andy Barosi, were to return immediately to the *Sarania*. This was quite frustrating, considering all he had been learning from Professor Cobler and his colleagues. However, he felt an urgent desire to go find Reese and see if she was okay.

Andy gave no additional information. Jason was torn. An order was an order. However, he could pretend he misunderstood the order. Professor Cobler had told him that Reese had left the university to go to agricultural biosphere 4115.

The sliptube capsule's hatch opened. He went to the control panel and inserted his passkey device. The menu of destinations appeared. He easily found Vlaera University, GovCenter and Drydock 168. He had to look a little harder to find biosphere 4115. He touched the indicator and confirmed the destination. He strapped into the acceleration couch and the capsule began to move. It should have been only a few minutes since 4115 was only supposed to be a few habitats away.

After half an hour he became concerned. It shouldn't have been this long. *Did I make a mistake?* He tried to access the touch screen again. But it was unresponsive. *Perhaps the controls lock during transit?*

After another hour, the capsule finally decelerated. The hatch opened. A man stood there, not floating as he had become accustomed to seeing in a sliptube station but actually standing with feet on a floor surface.

"Dr. Ford?" the man inquired.

104

"Yes."

"My name is Birn Girstanis. Welcome."

CHAPTER 12

Lyla watched three of Torg's crew attach a remote-control thruster unit on the far side of the asteroid. This thruster and five others would help adjust the momentum of the asteroid. The crew happened to have a pressure suit in Lyla's size so Torg had granted permission for her to join one of the "pinning gangs" on the surface. She was fascinated to see the use of explosive charges to drive anchor spikes into the rock.

First, they had to slow the spin of the rock. But they didn't want to slow it completely. The spin allowed them to apply correctional thrust from several angles. Once they approached the mining facility, they would have to overcome all momentum. All of this would be achieved using these remote thrusters.

In her earpiece, she could hear the sparse comments between the EVA crew. They were well-trained and focused. Suddenly, the communications officer cut in.

"Dr. Covarti, I have a call for you from the *Sarania*. Should I patch it through?"

"Go ahead."

"Lyla, this is Kai Herstonick."

"Kai, you're not going to believe where I am. I'm standing on the surface of an actual asteroid. It's amazing what these people do."

"I'm sure it is, Lyla. Unfortunately, Commander Enberg has issued a full crew recall order. All personnel are to return to the *Sarania* immediately."

"What? Why?"

"I'd rather not discuss it right now. You need to have Captain Torg bring you back immediately."

"That's not possible. They've already altered the trajectory of this asteroid. They are at a critical juncture."

"Lyla, this is an order from the Commander. I didn't want to say this over an open channel, but he and Reese Monsell have been attacked."

"Are they okay?"

"Yes, as far as I can tell. But they don't know who attacked them. Enberg wants the crew safe and secure on the *Sarania* until he can determine what's going on."

"Kai, if this crew doesn't finish its work, this asteroid will crash into the SolarSphere. Thousands of people could be killed. There's no need to worry about me. These are good people. They've looked out for me. They are the Spherian equivalent of fireweeders. And they're in the middle of a full burn, if you know what I mean."

"I understand. Ask anyway. I've got to contact the rest of the crew. Herstonick out."

○ ● ○ ● ○

Jason looked at the man *standing* in front of him at the sliptube station. There was no gravity, yet his feet seemed planted solidly on a surface that he judged as the floor.

"How are you not floating?" Jason asked Girstanis.

"It's quite simple, Dr. Ford. Our shoes have adherent soles, using subatomic forces."

Using the various handholds, Jason adjusted his body's orientation to match Girstanis's.

"How do you know who I am?" he asked.

"The news of the arrival of the *Sarania*," Girstanis said, "and its crew has spread throughout the Sphere."

"That may be, but how did you know I would be here at this exact moment?"

"I think you already suspect," Girstanis said, "that we remotely altered your sliptube capsule's destination."

"Why?"

"We wanted to meet you and offer you a gift, something you will want to share with your fellow Refugians."

"But why did I need to be diverted, just to receive a gift?" Jason asked. "I'm sorry, but I feel like I've been kidnapped."

"That is a reasonable conclusion," Girstanis said in an odd matter-of-fact tone, as if kidnapping was an unimportant matter. "But please understand, we mean you no harm. The urgency of our meeting was prompted by your Commander Enberg. He has recalled you and your crewmates back to your ship. We suspect after the events in the agricultural biosphere, we might lose the opportunity to meet any of you. And ours is a gift that may be misunderstood."

Jason observed Girstanis's face was completely expressionless. Someone offering a gift would usually be smiling. He looked around the sliptube station, noticing two other people—a man and a woman standing on either side of him—equally expressionless.

"We offer you," Girstanis continued, "the gift of logical and unemotional clarity. As a historian, you are familiar with numerous examples in which strife and pain were brought on by unbridled emotions, especially the emotions of those who possessed power. How many political leaders have manipulated the emotions of human populations with devastating results? This in turn leads to an emotional countermovement, in which another leader can proceed to do the same thing."

"The political pendulum," Jason said.

"I am not familiar with that metaphor," Girstanis said, "but it fits. Our mission is to end that cycle of suffering."

"And how do you plan to achieve such an ambitious task?" Jason asked, feeling a surreal oddness in having such an academic discussion with someone who had arranged to kidnap him. But Jason decided he should play along. "What social, economic or political system could accomplish such a miracle?"

"None," Girstanis said. "For the state of human affairs to change, humans must change. Emotional decisions must be eliminated."

"I don't see that happening anytime soon," Jason countered, "either here on the SolarSphere or on my world."

"It has already begun. I am one such example. We are the Logicus. We do not act out of greed, ego, lust, anger or any other emotional motivation. And we will give you that same capacity."

"As you said, our commander has recalled us," Jason said. "I believe it's only a temporary measure. We should be able to speak soon. I would love to hear more about your philosophy."

"We offer more than philosophy."

Suddenly, Girstanis's two aides grabbed his arms with iron-like grips.

○ ● ○ ● ○

"We need to get back to the *Sarania*," Enberg said, pacing back and forth in the examination room in a way that made Reese feel anxious.

"Are you planning to leave the Sphere?" Trin asked.

"Not necessarily. I need reports from my crew about their experiences. I also hope your security people will find the man who assaulted me. I'd like to know if I was specifically targeted and why?"

"Perhaps," Trin ventured, "it was a random attack."

"A man waits in a restricted zero-G area so he can randomly attack a stranger? Do you normally have random attacks on the SolarSphere?"

One of the security guards entered the room.

"Pardon me, Minister Trin," the guard said. "We have a priority message for you."

"Excuse me, Commander," Trin said. "It's probably President Maklund wanting to know if you're all right."

Enberg nodded.

"Do you think it might be time to leave the Sphere?" Reese asked.

Enberg just shrugged.

When Trin came back she looked pale.

"You wanted to return to your ship? Let's not delay. Your safety is our primary concern."

The medical officer gave Enberg a cane to aid him in walking. The three of them were escorted to the sliptube station by a security patrol. Enberg looked back at the octagonal hatch, which led to the Great Tree.

"Whatever happened to Professor Flessik?" he asked.

"Who?" Trin asked.

"She escorted me here from the university," Reese said.

"I'm not sure," Trin said. "I expect our investigators will track her down for questioning, if they haven't already."

Trin motioned them into the sliptube capsule. The security guards were about to join them in the sliptube, but Trin waved them off.

"We're going straight to our destination," she said. "You won't be needed. Report to the investigators. Offer them any assistance you can."

Once Trin entered the destination into the control panel, she seemed oddly quiet.

"Is everything okay?" Reese asked after a few minutes.

"What does 'okay' mean?" Trin asked.

"It means all right. You seem distracted. Is everything all right?"

"Ah," she said, nodding her head. "Have you ever had a conflict in your duties?"

"I'm not exactly sure what you mean," Reese said.

"I've been loyal to Pegg Maklund for years, even before she was elected president. She's a good woman, a superb leader, someone you can trust."

"Well, she certainly has been very welcoming to us," Reese agreed.

"And she's very upset that the Commander has been attacked," Trin said, looking over at Enberg.

"But," Enberg interjected, "I also know she has an ulterior motive."

"And what's that?" Trin asked.

"You may already know. But she asked me not to discuss it."

Trin looked at him quizzically. "This has something to do with her taking you to the empty habitat, doesn't it? She's keeping secrets."

"Don't you find most people do?" Enberg said, smiling. "Especially politicians. No offense."

"You said you were loyal to Maklund," Reese said, "but in a way that suggests you have a loyalty elsewhere."

"Yes," Trin said. "I must confess I'm not taking you directly back to Drydock 168. There are some other people who need to speak with you."

"So I guess you have secrets, too."

○ ● ○ ● ○

Girstanis and his companions forced Jason to the elevator and they descended. He could feel the artificial gravity starting to take effect. He had to think of a way to escape.

"Could you release me? There is no place for me to run in this elevator. And they're hurting my arms."

"Release him," Girstanis said.

"Thank you."

Jason knew there was no way he could overpower these people, especially in such an enclosed space, even if he had any martial arts skills. He would need to escape after they left the elevator. He needed to delay whatever they were going to do with him. Would it be possible to gain their trust before then?

"I wish to apologize for my reaction…to your offer."

"No apology is needed," Girstanis said. "Your reaction was similar to your fellow emotives."

Again, Jason was struck by the flatness of Girstanis's delivery.

"Emotives?"

"Those who react emotionally. In other words, anyone who has not undergone our process."

"And they all respond negatively to your offer?"

"Always."

"Wouldn't it be useful to be able to avoid such a response?" Jason asked.

"No such strategy exists," Girstanis answered.

"That you know of," Jason said. "Can you say for sure such a strategy does not exist?"

"In this case it would be a logical fallacy to say we can prove such a negative."

"What if I were to help you develop such a strategy?" Jason asked. "As a sympathetic emotive, I would be in a unique position to help develop such a strategy."

"This is more likely a tactic to delay your processing."

"Not at all. I have suffered from my emotions my entire lifetime. Anger and disappointment at being passed over. Unrequited love. Lost love. These are all bitter feelings, which I shall be relieved to be rid of."

"And we will assist you to do that," Girstanis said.

"And I look forward to that. But in the meantime while I am still an emotive, I would like to repay the service you are about to do for me."

"While such an exploration might be fruitful, there is a concern over the time you will be away from your crew and the suspicion that time would generate."

"Among my crew I have a reputation for enthusiastic curiosity. I have already disobeyed my commander by not returning directly to our ship. Any further delay can be explained by that curiosity."

"How would you suggest we proceed?" Girstanis asked.

The elevator door opened.

Jason looked out. This habitat was not the open architecture of Vlaera or GovCenter. It looked older without any notable aesthetics, completely utilitarian.

"Perhaps a tour to start," Jason suggested.

"I fail to understand how a physical tour would contribute to developing an effective persuasion strategy."

"That is because you are not—what did call me—an emotive."

"We were all emotives once," Girstanis said.

Jason's mind focused on countering Girstanis's logic. His life, his very identity, depended on it.

"I was a child once," he said. "And even though I can remember what it was like to be a child, I can't necessarily predict how a child will react."

"There is a tenuous logic to your analogy," Girstanis said. "However, I believe it is still likely you are attempting to find a way to avert your processing."

"However, if you are wrong," Jason said, "you will have lost an opportunity that cannot be recovered. Even if I were trying to avoid the process, you would still impose it on me. What do you have to lose?"

"Time."

There was no more negotiating with Girstanis. As hard as he resisted, Jason could feel the fight-or-flight response welling up inside him. His heartbeat was increasing. He could feel his blood pressure rising. He pushed Girstanis aside and began running down the long corridor.

"Retrieve him," Girstanis said to his two associates.

Jason could hear the two Logicus running after him. He looked back briefly to see his lead increasing. His adrenaline might have given him an advantage. He turned down another corridor, then yet another one to lose his pursuers.

He then came to a T-intersection. People were on either side. However, they were ignoring him, at least for the moment. He assumed they were Logicus who were unaware of his escape.

Jason decided to turn right. He walked past two technicians attending to a piece of equipment. They didn't even look up as he passed. He walked briskly but hopefully not so fast that he would attract attention. He would try to circle around to the other side of the elevator shaft. There would probably be a guard or sentry, but he would have to deal with that when he got there.

He turned another corner to discover a sight he couldn't quite comprehend. At first he thought it was a man in an elaborate pressure suit, but then realized the arms and legs were in no way human, completely mechanical. It was grotesque, a human body integrated into a robotic body. The prosthetics extended far beyond the limbs. How much he couldn't tell.

Is this what they intend for me?

Chapter 13

Enberg, Trin and Reese floated out of the sliptube capsule into the station.

"Where are you taking us?" Enberg demanded.

"To see one of the most important men in the SolarSphere."

"And who exactly is that?" Reese asked.

"The head of our order," Trin said.

"Your order?" Enberg said. "Presumably, this order, whatever it is, falls outside the SolarSphere's government."

"Yes," Trin admitted.

"We didn't travel hundreds of light years to involve ourselves in someone else's political intrigues, especially given our recent experience at the tree."

"I promise you are completely safe here," Trin said.

"And if we weren't safe, would you tell us?" Enberg asked.

Reese had never seen Enberg look so grim.

Trin frowned. "Commander, I know trust is difficult at this point," she said. "But I could have made up some pretext for coming here. I could have lied to you, filling in rational and convincing details. Isn't that what you'd expect from us politicians? It's important you meet this man without Maklund knowing, at least for now. It's not political, at least in any sense you might think. But it is vital."

Enberg's silence indicated he was still not convinced.

"Commander," Trin said. "You have your passkeys. You can leave via sliptube at any time. Remember, I sent the security guards away. There is no one here to stop you from leaving. The choice is yours."

Reese stepped next to Trin. "Commander, I think we can trust her."

Enberg nodded. "All right. For now."

Trin led them into the lift. Once they arrived at the ground level, they followed Trin along a corridor a few hundred feet. She stopped at a non-descript, unmarked door.

Once inside, they found an older hunched-over man waiting for them. For someone who was possibly "the most important man in the SolarSphere," Reese didn't think he looked particularly impressive. Behind him stood a tall man with perfect posture and a bland expression, providing a stark contrast and making the older man look even less significant.

"Sister Trin, it is good to see you again," the old man said. "It has been too long. But I know our First Minister doesn't have much time to spare."

"Brother," she said, "I'd like to introduce Commander Garris Enberg and Dr. Reese Monsell of the *Sarania*."

The old man nodded and stepped forward.

"Welcome. My name is Dr. Edwis Yurasti. Most call me Brother Yurasti. This is Brother Maynberc. While I deeply admire your courage and envy the adventure you've undertaken, I had hoped we'd never meet. Or more specifically, I hoped the need would never arise."

"Then why are we meeting?" Enberg asked, looking at Trin. "Why have we been diverted to see you?"

"It's complicated." Yurasti sighed. "Let's take some refreshment," he said, gesturing to a door on the other side of the room.

Reese noticed Yurasti walked awkwardly. It looked painful, but the old man didn't even wince.

Once inside they all sat down around a work table. Reese looked around the dingy room. It was filled with consoles, monitors and other equipment. Only a metal cot and blanket at the other end of the room suggested anyone actually lived there.

Maynberc served them each a beverage. Both Reese and Enberg waited for the others to drink before they did the same. Their suspicions were high.

Normally, Reese would have asked about the origin of the beverage, but there were more important matters at hand.

"We know who attacked you at the Great Tree," Yurasti said.

"So quickly? Who?" Enberg asked.

"While I don't know the name of the specific individual, he was a member of a very dangerous faction, fanatics who follow an extreme dogma. And you and your crew have drawn their attention. They believe humanity must be purged of all emotions."

"All right," Enberg said, "but it still doesn't explain why they would they attack me."

"It wasn't an assault in the conventional sense," Yurasti said. "It was an attempted kidnapping."

"For some sort of ransom? Or to make a statement of some kind?"

"Neither." Yurasti leaned forward. "We believe they wanted to inflict their process on you."

"What process?"

"This faction has developed a method of forcibly removing emotions from a person's cognitive processes. The procedure involves electro-neurological stimulation and surgery. They operate on the amygdala, the part of the brain responsible for emotions."

Reese and Enberg were quiet, absorbing this unexpected information. Reese felt a certain dread. *Why is this secretive order sharing this information with us?*

"Well, luckily for me, their kidnapping attempt failed." Enberg turned to Trin. "It makes me want to return to our ship as soon as possible. It is not our mission to get involved in your society's conflicts."

"Yes, I agree," Yurasti said. "However, if that were the end of the story, we wouldn't be sitting here. But unfortunately, they've seized another member of your crew."

"Who?"

"You will find the only unaccounted member of your crew is Dr. Ford."

"Jason?" Reese said. "How do you know they have him?"

"President Maklund gave each member of your crew a passkey to operate the sliptube system, correct?"

"Yes," Enberg said. "Let me guess. The passkey also serves as a tracking device."

"I'm afraid so. And *they* have hacked into the passkey system. So have we, as a matter of fact. The transponder code for Dr. Ford's passkey disappeared from the system. He was traveling from Vlaera University to the agro biosphere where you were attacked, but he never arrived. Then the transponder signal disappeared. He became untraceable, even by us.

"With the sheer size of the SolarSphere," Reese said, "we'll never find him. We might never see him again."

"No," Yurasti said. "You will see him again. But he won't be the same. He will be devoid of all emotion, although he will be able to imitate them as necessary to maintain his cover."

"What do you mean, *maintain his cover*?" Enberg asked.

"When he returns to you, he will have a mission to convert the Refugian population to the same unemotional state, just as the Logicus are trying to do on the Sphere. That's what they call themselves, the Logicus. I said they are fanatics. It wasn't until your attempted abduction that we suspected their ambition extended beyond the SolarSphere. Dr. Ford's capture confirmed it."

Enberg looked down pensively. "Having control over one's emotions doesn't seem that extreme, certainly not something to fight a war over."

"But it is not controlling emotions," Yurasti said, "but the complete elimination of them. One does not simply lose hate, anger, envy and sadness; one also loses joy, love and compassion. And you lose something even more important: guilt."

"Guilt?" Reese asked. "Why is that so vital?"

"Guilt is the emotional component of conscience. Without a conscience, we become psychopaths or sociopaths. Without conscience, we can commit horrible transgressions as long as we have a logical motive. Right and wrong become obsolete concepts. Utilitarianism replaces morality."

"Ends justify means," Enberg said.

"Exactly. The Logicus have gone far beyond mere psychopathology."

"Even so," Enberg said, "Jason has always been loyal to our mission, to our crew. How does this process make him betray all that?"

"Admittedly, there is an indoctrination element to the process, but it doesn't take much. You see, loyalty is an emotion, too. From Dr. Ford's perspective, he will be trying to help your people."

"Is there a treatment?" Reese asked. "A way to undo this procedure?"

"No," Yurasti said, "the process is irreversible. We have studied the matter in great depth. So now we are warning you, so you can take precautions to protect your planet."

"I'm not sure how the conversion of one man is really a threat to Refugia."

Yurasti smiled a crooked yet kindly smile. "Never underestimate the combination of fanaticism and intelligence. And the Logicus have both." He leaned forward. "Suppose I could offer you a prosthetic arm, superior to your own arm in every way? Would you be willing to have your own healthy arm amputated?"

Reese and Enberg looked at each other, caught off guard at this odd change of subject.

"Of course not," Enberg answered.

"Why not?" Yurasti asked.

"My arm is perfectly good as it is."

"But the arm being offered would be superior in every way. Yet, you still wouldn't amputate your own arm, correct?"

Enberg nodded.

"Your decision is an emotional one," Yurasti said. "Yet, I understand it because, like you, I am human. As you can see my deformed body could benefit from physical enhancements, but I dare not."

"Why not?" Reese asked.

"The Logicus have infiltrated much of SolarSphere society, particularly surgical centers."

"Maynberc," Yurasti said, "would you show our guests your arm?"

Maynberc stepped forward and pulled up his sleeve, revealing an arm covered in artificial skin. He peeled back the skin to reveal the cybernetic components underneath.

"Both of his arms are artificial. His legs as well. With the strength of his limbs, Maynberc could easily crush anyone of us. Or all of us."

"You're a Logicus?" Enberg asked.

"No," Yurasti said. "He is a victim of the Logicus. From their perspective, Maynberc's processing was a failure, a misfire they call it. While he is incapable of experiencing any emotion, for some reason he has retained a conscience. Because of his unusual situation, he has made an extraordinarily valuable operative."

"I cannot feel joy," Maynberc admitted. "And while I am not capable of regretting the loss, I understand on an intellectual level what the Logicus did to me was wrong. It was a violation of my civil rights, my humanity. They didn't realize my sense of morality was still in place. I don't understand how myself. I was injured in an accident. A doctor—a secret Logicus—offered to replace my injured arm with a cybernetic one. I agreed. But they also performed their neurological procedure without my permission. Once they replaced one arm, they thought it only logical to replace all my limbs."

"Do all of the victims have their limbs replaced?" Reese asked.

"No," Maynberc said, "but if it would benefit their particular mission, they have no objection. To them, it is only logical. As Brother Yurasti said, many have infiltrated SolarSphere society. They are normal in all physical ways. Only a neurological scan would reveal their alteration."

"We believe," Yurasti added, "Professor Flessik, the woman who led you to the Great Tree, is one of those, a non-cyborg Logicus."

"She seemed quite normal to me," Reese said, "unlike Brother Maynberc here." She then realized the insult she may have given. She looked to Maynberc. "No offense."

"Offense is an emotional reaction," Maynberc said. "Therefore, none is possible for me."

"Unlike Maynberc whose processing was thankfully imperfect," Yurasti said, "we assume Dr. Ford will be quite able to imitate emotion, just as Professor Flessik had. But, on the other hand, there are those who have had significant body alterations, even greater than Maynberc's."

Yurasti activated an image on one of his view screens.

Reese cringed in horror. On the screen was an image of a person inside some manner of pressure suit. However, instead of arms and legs, there were mechanical appendages.

"Obviously," Yuratsi said, "this individual has been altered for work in the vacuum of space."

A chill ran through Reese's spine.

"But they won't do this to Jason?" Reese asked, hoping for reassurance. "Right?"

"They could, but our analysis suggests his mission will be to infiltrate your society. For that, he would need to be physically unchanged."

"How many Logicus are there?" Enberg asked.

"We estimate over 200,000," Yuratsi said. "Their numbers are small compared to the Sphere's population, but they are growing at an accelerated rate."

Enberg turned to Nysandra Trin. "And President Maklund knows nothing of this?"

"No," Trin said. "And I must see that it stays that way. If you'll excuse me,   I've been gone too long." With that, Trin walked out the door.

"I guess there's no better spy on the President than her own First Minister."

"Don't get us wrong," Yurasti continued. "President Maklund is a good leader…in general. She's an excellent consensus builder and negotiator. Her diplomatic skills are superb. Very inclusive. But she would try to embrace the Logicus as friends and negotiate with them. There is no negotiating with the Logicus. So, for the sake of your people, it would be better for Dr. Ford to never return to Refugia. The Logicus are like a virus, an intelligent, adaptable and fanatical virus. And soon Dr. Ford will be a Logicus."

"How long does this process take?" Enberg asked.

"The initial psychological conditioning," Maynberc said, "using precise electro-neural stimulation, can vary between two and six hours. The surgical procedure is only an hour. However, once the first phase is complete, the process is irreversible."

○ ● ○ ● ○

Jason backed away from the grotesque cyborg ahead of him. As he turned the next corner, Girstanis's female associate grabbed his arms. Despite her being several inches shorter, Jason was no match for her strength. He realized she was a cyborg too, just not as significantly as the monster he had just seen.

"What have they done to you?" he asked.

"I have been freed of painful and counterproductive emotions. I am achieving a higher portion of my potential and contributing to a better world."

"I'm sorry for your loss," he said.

"Sorrow is irrelevant and wasteful."

"She is correct, Dr. Ford," Girstanis said as he walked toward them. "Piran, take Dr. Ford to the processing suite immediately. I believe Bay 43 is available."

Jason tried again to break free of Piran, but struggling was useless. The harder he pulled away from her, the tighter and more painful her grip became.

"Don't damage him," Girstanis said before walking away.

Piran firmly dragged Jason down a corridor.

"Piran, what were you like before you were transformed?"

"Emotional."

"Don't you miss it? I mean the joy. Love? Family?"

At this point Piran pulled Jason into a room that only intensified his fear. At the center of this room full of monitors and consoles was a couch with restraints.

"You will have no pain when you wake up," she said.

These were the last words Jason heard as the two other iron-gripped beings strapped him down on the treatment couch.

CHAPTER 14

Reese looked around at the others sitting at the table in Yurasti's room.

"We need to rescue Jason," she insisted.

Yurasti sighed. "I regret to say that is impossible."

Reese felt a horrible pain in the pit of her stomach.

"Why is it impossible?" Enberg asked.

"The likelihood of success is extremely remote," Yurasti explained. "And if your attempt failed, you would be captured. Then you would become one of them, making the situation that much worse. We would need to contact your second-in-command and explain what we have explained to you. Then upon your return she—I believe her name is Kai Herstonick—would need to stage a mutiny against you. Mutinies are messy affairs, often prone to failure."

"I'm willing to take that chance," Enberg said.

"But I am not," Yurasti snapped. "You now know of our operations. If captured, you would reveal them to the Logicus."

"I don't know what your operations are," Enberg said. "All I can tell is you are fighting some kind of covert war. On my planet, we fight against the fireweed, not technically a war but close. Among fireweeders, we believe in *no one left behind*."

"I appreciate that," Yurasti said, "but your capture would alert them to our existence and the surveillance we conduct. And that, I cannot permit. As I've said, their extreme fanaticism must never leave the SolarSphere for the sake of your own planet, for the sake of your people. Like your fireweed, it must not be allowed to spread. You can stop Ford when he reappears. But could your loyal crew stop you if you were converted to a Logicus?"

At that moment the door opened. Symas Graith stepped through.

"Brother Graith?" Yurasti seemed disturbed by Graith's sudden presence. "What brings you here?"

Graith looked at Enberg and Reese with a surprised expression.

"Brother Yurasti," Graith said. "Why have you brought the Refugians here?"

"One of their crew has been taken by the Logicus," Yurasti explained.

There was a pained expression on Graith's face. He looked to Enberg.

"I'm sorry for your loss." Graith seemed quite sincere.

"He's not dead," Reese said a bit louder than she intended.

"I'm afraid he will be shortly," Graith said.

"What do you mean?" Yurasti demanded.

"We are initiating final sanction."

"What?" Yurasti said. "Why now?"

"The alignment of our assets is optimal. If we miss this window, it may be years before we get another chance. Think of all the innocent people who will be processed in that time. Your last report indicated a higher percentage of Logicus are in Sector L at this very moment." Graith leaned forward over the table. "Yurasti, you are a brilliant spymaster, but it is now time for decisive action."

"We don't have enough explosives in place yet," Yurasti countered. "The loss of Preldon Krelnikoff has set us back. This was not approved."

"I don't need your approval. I have four darkships in position, fully loaded. It is time."

○ ● ○ ● ○

The fog rose. Jason found himself standing on the Outer Scorch on Refugia. *How did I get here?* Then the smell hit him. He remembered it from his mandatory service in the fireweeders. Burning fireweed—the stench actually more from the accelerant the flame guns used.

"You know, smell is the most memory-evocative sense we have," a voice from behind him said.

He turned around to see Reese. Her shoes were on fire, but she didn't seem to mind. She bent over, picked up some fireweed and put it in a pot. Flames burst out of the pot.

"Finally, a vegetable that cooks itself."

She smiled. Jason never realized how beautiful her smile was before. But he knew something was wrong. Jason wasn't here; he was somewhere else. *Where?* It was a dark place, a cold place. *This is not real.* Then breaking his reverie was a harsh voice, cutting into his mind like a knife.

"Here on the Outer Scorch, you couldn't cut it, could you?" said a distinctively high and nasal voice. "Could you, Ford?"

Jason turned to see Damian Quertsa, the Director General of the Space Administration, the same man who tried to block his inclusion on the *Sarania* mission.

"You couldn't cut it with the fireweeders," Quertsa continued. "So how could we trust you on a mission to Earth?"

"I served my time with the fireweeders without complaint," Jason said.

"Served your time?" Quertsa taunted, "Like a prison sentence? How many burn runs did you go on?"

"Several."

"Three! Only three!" Quertsa snapped.

"I did my duty," Jason said. "I provided support for my team at the base camp."

"Leaders don't support. *Leaders lead!* Right, Garris? Of course, they do. The Enbergs were an old fireweeder family, three generations I believe. Garris here was raised on the Outer Scorch. He became a pilot, not for glory but to burn the weed on the high Red Cliffs." Quertsa turned back to Enberg shaking his head. "He could take the heat!"

"Others just melt," Enberg said, pointing at Jason's feet. "See!"

Jason's feet were indeed dissolving. His ankles were standing in a puddle of goo. He wondered why he didn't get any shorter. He looked deeper into the translucent goo. There was a pile of old paperbound books where his feet had been. He looked up at Enberg again, who was now kissing Reese quite passionately.

"No!" Jason yelled. "Stop, I love her!"

Enberg pulled his head back but continued to look at Reese.

"Love? What an odd thing to say. Did you ever commit?" Enberg asked. "Did you ever tell her you love her?"

"He never did," Reese said, shaking her head. "Maybe he's still carrying a torch for Jennika?"

"Who's Jennika?" Enberg asked.

"That's his old girlfriend back on Refugia," Quertsa explained, "the one he left behind, discarded like a used tissue."

A wave of long-forgotten guilt rose up, striking Jason like a tidal wave. His chest felt tighten. He hadn't thought of Jennika in a long time, not since before they arrived at the Sphere.

"You do know she's dead now?" Reese asked.

"Of course, he does," Quertsa said, "even if she lived to be a hundred years. She'll certainly be dead by time the *Sarania* returns home. You know, all that time dilation between twists."

"Think he feels guilty about her?" Enberg asked.

"Hmm, is that why he won't commit to me?" Reese asked.

"We're shipmates," Jason called out in his defense, breathing heavily.

"Did you ever tell Reese you love her?" Quertsa asked from behind Jason.

Jason suddenly recalled Quertsa's bad breath, another memory-evocative smell. He turned to see the Director General smiling smugly.

"Did you ever have the guts to jump into the unknown?" Quertsa demanded.

"I volunteered for the *Sarania* mission," Jason countered.

Quertsa snickered and turned up his lip in disdain.

"Did you ever have the guts to really burn the fireweed?" Enberg asked.

"Or tell me you love me?" Reese added.

Jason didn't know whom he wanted to punch more, Quertsa or Enberg. But if he walked off his book pedestal, he'd get shorter. He wouldn't be a match for either of them.

"That's you," Quertsa called out as if reading Jason's mind. "Afraid. And you wanted to be a commander?"

"Leadership is not always about being assigned command," Jason yelled back.

"Isn't it?" Quertsa asked, looking from Reese to Enberg, then back at Jason. "Then why did you want to command the *Sarania*? You? A historian? A dusty academic? An egghead? An imposter? You want all the facts *before* making a decision. You hide behind your curiosity, never crossing a bridge unless you know exactly what's on the other side. Curiosity without risk-taking. I mean curiosity is good and all that, but—"

"Guts are better!" Enberg said.

○ ● ○ ● ○

Captain Torg was completing the final handoff of the asteroid to Processing Plant N422.

"You're not bringing the asteroid all the way into the plant?" Lyla asked.

"No, we've handed control of the remote thrusters to the plant's Intake Control. They'll need to make very subtle maneuvers to bring the rock into their stable. They can do that as well or better than we can."

"Captain," the communications officer called out. "We have another call for Dr. Covarti from the *Sarania*."

"Do you want to take it in your quarters?" Torg asked.

"No, we have no secrets." Lyla pressed the contact. "Covarti here."

"Lyla, it's Kai Herstonick. You should have finished your asteroid mission by now. Correct?"

"We're finishing up now."

"Okay. Return to the *Sarania* immediately."

"Have they found whoever attacked the Commander?"

"Negative. Now he, Reese and Jason are missing."

"What?" Lyla said. "How long have they been missing?"

"Over five hours."

"According to protocol, that makes you acting commander."

"Yeah," Kai said, "until we can find the commander. Everyone else is on board except you."

"We should be out searching for them."

"I'd love to, but have you seen the size of this place?" Kai asked. "I've been in contact with President Maklund. She's having her people search. They can search far more effectively than we can. How soon can you get back here?"

"I'll need to consult with Captain Torg," Reese said. "She's right here with me."

"Commander Herstonick, this is Captain Torg. Good to speak to you again. Wish it was under better conditions. If I dock at the processing plant, Lyla can be back to you in 12 to 14 hours via sliptube. However, given that we don't know what's happening to your people, I suggest we bring her directly back to Drydock 168 on board my ship."

"But the dry dock is all sealed up with us inside."

"Yes, but there's an auxiliary airlock adjacent to the bay. We can easily dock with it. Right now, Dr. Covarti's well-being is my responsibility and I want to bring her home to you safe and sound."

"Thank you, Captain. That's acceptable and appreciated. Herstonick out."

Torg turned to her bridge crew.

"Navigation, set a course to Drydock 168."

○ ● ○ ● ○

Reese considered what Graith had just revealed. He was going to attack the section of the Sphere that held the Logicus, a place they called Sector L, with four of what he called "darkships." The name suggested these ships would be difficult to detect. Reese realized the disagreement between Graith and Yurasti wasn't going to stop the attack. Assuming the attack was successful, Jason would die with all the Logicus.

"We must rescue Jason before then," Reese said.

"I agree," said Enberg. "And it's my right to try to rescue my crew member."

"Even under ordinary circumstances," Yurasti said, glaring at Graith, "the probability of your Dr. Ford being successfully rescued is extremely remote. While we do know the sector they operate from, with the attack imminent it would be suicidal."

"We must try!" Reese snapped.

"Easy there," Enberg said. He turned to Yurasti. "You said you didn't want us to enter the Logicus's habitat because we might reveal your existence. Right?"

"Yes."

"If the attack is imminent," Enberg said, "then the need for secrecy no longer exists."

Yurasti nodded. "I suppose that is true. Although no outcome is guaranteed."

Enberg turned to Graith. "How long before your darkships strike?"

"Five and a half hours."

"That means," Enberg said, "I have five and a half hours to rescue Jason."

"A rescue would not be possible in the time remaining," Graith said. "It would take three hours just to get into Sector L. And once in the habitat, you would have to rescue your man while avoiding detection. Highly improbable. And understand this: The sliptube access to Sector L will be taken offline as a part of the attack."

"Regrettably," Yurasti said, "it seems your man is lost."

"Not necessarily," Maynberc said. "There may still be a way."

"How?" Enberg demanded.

"Prior to the connection of the sliptubes, travel pods are used to enter and exit a new habitat. Sector L is an older habitat. The pods are not compatible with newer infrastructure so they are mostly forgotten."

"So we can slip in and out probably unnoticed," Enberg said.

"Unlikely but it is possible."

"Commander Enberg cannot," Yurasti interrupted. "He is known. His picture with President Maklund has been circulated around the Sphere. The kidnapping attempt at the Great Tree indicates the Logicus have identified and desire him. He cannot enter Sector L. Our operation cannot be endangered. In addition, his leg injury makes the probability of success much lower."

"I don't need the damn cane. I can walk."

"But can you run if needed?"

"But I could go," Reese said. "No one cares about a biologist or cook."

"No," Enberg said, "you don't have the skills."

"No offense, Commander," Reese said, "but how many times have you infiltrated a hostile space station?"

Enberg became stone-faced.

"It is a moot point," Yurasti said. "Under no circumstances will we allow you to enter Sector L. Commander Enberg is a target. While Dr. Monsell could go, she is unlikely to succeed."

"Unless she has my assistance," Maynberc said.

CHAPTER 15

Jason was still standing on the Outer Scorch. The sun projected more waves of guilt and angst than heat. Breathing was not painful but labored. More family, friends, rivals and enemies had arrived to torment him. Quertsa stood there shaking his head, disapprovingly at every encounter. Why had a man he hadn't seen in years, who probably died long ago, become his master of torment? Jason never realized how much he hated Quertsa. He didn't recall ever feeling as much contempt for this man as he did right at this moment. An acidic bile filled his throat. He turned away from the crowd to see Reese.

"Reese, help me," Jason pleaded. "You of all people need to be on my side."

"Your side?" Reese asked. "What side are you on?"

"Our side. The mission's," Jason said. "I—"

They small crowd began chanting, "I, I, I, I, I—." Each syllable was a stab to his sanity.

"I believe in the mission!" he shouted over the taunting chorus.

Again, they began to chant in an annoying child-like, sing-song cadence, "The mission, the mission, that's just you wish'n."

"Help you?" Reese asked. "Maybe you should ask Jennika. You know, the woman you abandoned."

Suddenly from behind Reese stepped Jennika Burlaine, the woman he had loved, but left behind on Refugia. Seeing her stand there, Jason had almost forgotten her beautiful dark brown eyes for which no photograph could do justice.

"You told me you loved me," Jennika said. "We were going to build a life together. But then you left me behind. For what? A dead planet?"

"Jenn, I'm sorry," Jason said as beads of perspiration slid down the side of his face. "The *Sarania* mission to Earth was a once-in-a-lifetime opportunity."

"I was a once-in-a-lifetime opportunity," Jennika said as she placed her hand on his cheek. Her warm hand turned ice cold. "But I'm dead now. I was the sacrifice on the altar of your ambition." She turned away from him. "So there's no more Jennika for you to come back to. When you return to Refugia, you can come and dance on my grave if you like."

"Wow," Reese added. "Talk about commitment issues. I thought it was just me you wouldn't commit to."

"Men!" Jennika said, smirking. "Who needs them?"

Then she and Reese walked off, making room for others to move in and torment him in a montage of guilt and grievances.

"Why couldn't you help? Where were you when I needed you? How couldn't you support your mentor? You didn't keep my secret!" The flood of accusations peppered his mind with guilt.

Then, from the corner of his eye, Jason saw an older woman he didn't recognize. He noticed her primarily because she wasn't taunting him. She had a curious expression on her face. Was this woman someone he had failed but had forgotten? She was dressed in a fashion Jason didn't recognize, nothing like a Refugian or Spherian. She was silently observing Jason's crowd of tormentors.

Jason proceeded to hear variations of every argument he ever had with anyone. Some arguments had been long forgotten. Old wounds were now reopened, both small and large. Jason finally fell to his knees, his hands landing on the hot burning sand.

"Shut up, shut up!" he yelled, but none yielded. He was losing control of his mind. Their words became deafening. He wanted to rip out his ears. He wanted to die.

Finally, the mysterious woman started to walk closer. She pushed the other people aside quite easily.

"Quiet your mind," she whispered, but her whisper somehow registered louder than all the other voices combined. Her accent was unlike any he had heard before. It wasn't Refugian. And he had not heard that accent on the SolarSphere, at least not yet.

Who are you? Jason thought.

"Quiet your mind," she repeated. A pleasant coolness radiated from her words.

"It's not easy," Jason cried. "They won't shut up!"

"They have nothing to say that you want to hear. You know that. Breathe. Focus on your breathing. Silence them with your will. They are not here. This is all in your mind. Our captors want you to hate those emotions you're feeling. Concentrate on my voice."

His breathing became easier. All the other voices started to blend together into unintelligible white noise.

"Who are you?" he asked, slowly standing up.

"Most recently, I've been called 908. But the important question is who are you?"

"You're in my dream, this nightmare," he said, looking up at the woman. "You should know my name."

"This is not a dream," she said, "at least not in the strictest sense. It's an induced mental state, closer to hypnosis but much deeper. I am from outside your consciousness."

"Girstanis," he snarled, finally remembering being strapped down onto the couch. He pulled away from her. "You work for Girstanis!"

The buzz of the others around him got louder again.

"No," the woman said, "I'm also a prisoner of the Logicus but in a different way from you. Girstanis thinks I'm cooperating with him. And he doesn't know I'm here. I've tunneled into your mindspace."

Jason stepped back from her, squinting to see her better. "Into my what?"

"I've hacked into the system the Logicus are using to manipulate your mind," she said. "We are both prisoners, but we can help each other."

"I don't understand."

The buzz of voices started to increase further. Jason looked around at all the people surrounding him. Their voices were becoming distinct again.

"Focus on me," she said as touched her palm to his cheek. It was a gentle touch, a calming touch. "Girstanis and his kind are trying to cause you so much emotional pain you'll subconsciously be willing to do anything to free yourself from those emotions. They are trying to reprogram your subconscious and make it surrender to their way of thinking. Girstanis and his people have already purged their own feelings. They believe it's a superior way to live, so much so, they want to inflict it on the rest of humanity—whether they are willing or not."

"Girstanis told me about that," Jason said, starting to recall Girstanis's words before being strapped onto the couch. "I vaguely remember my conversation with him." He slowly looked away. "How do I know you aren't part of this process of theirs?"

"The fact I told you it was a process and not a dream should carry some weight. I want you to resist them. I want you to save yourself. And maybe save me too. What's your name?" she asked.

"Jason Ford."

"Jason, that's a nice name." She turned and looked around. "Where are we?" she asked, waving her hand at their surroundings.

"It's called the Outer Scorch," Jason said, recalling the boredom and misery it represented. But he supposed that was the point if what this woman said was true.

"What's the Outer Scorch?" she asked.

"A place I'd gladly thought I'd left behind." Jason chuckled darkly. "It's a rather unpleasant area of my home planet."

"Earth?"

"No, Refugia."

"So we're actually on another planet?" The woman seemed amazed.

"You say *another* planet. What planet are you from?"

"Earth," she said as if it were obvious. "Where are we? I don't mean this scorch place. I mean in physical reality. Where is your body?"

"On the SolarSphere."

"What's that?" she asked.

How could she not know? Was this a trick?

"What's the SolarSphere?" she repeated.

"It's a superstructure, orbiting the Earth's sun, an incomplete Dyson sphere." While it seemed odd for Jason to have to explain this, another possibility occurred to him. "So there are people *still* living on Earth?"

She shrugged. "I have no idea."

○ ● ○ ● ○

Maynberc brought Reese to a room with two rows of 12 oblong hatches on the floor. These were very different from the octagonal hatches Reese was used to seeing around the Sphere. She suspected this section represented an earlier generation of Sphere architecture.

"I was surprised that Graith and Yurasti are allowing us to go to Sector L," Reese said.

"As Brother Yurasti agreed with Commander Enberg," Maynberc said, "that once the attack comes, the need for secrecy will no longer be necessary. And if you die, you will be an even smaller problem for Director Graith to deal with."

"Typical politician," Reese snorted. "But if we are probably going to die, why are you coming with us?"

"The probabilities cannot be calculated," Maynberc said. "However, without me you would definitely fail. Besides, without emotions, I no longer have a fear of death."

"Regardless, I thank you," Reese said. "You're very brave."

"Incorrect. Without fear there is no courage," Maynberc said. "We must hurry. When the attack comes, access to the sliptube network will be severed. However, we do have external maintenance pods."

Maynberc gestured to the oblong hatches on the floor.

"Each hatch leads to a travel pod. They were originally used as transportation for workers to get to a habitat before it was brought online and connected to the rest of the sphere. They are old but functional. They have docking mechanisms compatible with the hatches of the older Sector L."

Maynberc opened the hatches to two of the pods and started to power up their systems.

"I've encrypted the comm systems," Maynberc said, "so we can communicate with each other, but no one else will be able to hear us."

"Each of these looks like they can hold two people," Reese observed. "Why are we taking two pods?" Enberg asked.

"If we are to recover Dr. Ford, we will need the capacity to bring him back. Do you feel comfortable piloting a travel pod?"

"It's okay," Reese said. "I've trained on the landers. And docking was easy compared to landing."

"Very well."

"Maynberc," Reese asked, "is there someone else you hope to rescue?"

"Other than Dr. Ford I have no expectations of rescuing anyone specific. However, if there is someone else who has not completed the process, it would be only logical to rescue them as well."

"Do you have family or friends among the Logicus?"

"My wife," Maynberc said. "She was injured in the same accident that I was. However, unlike myself, she was successfully processed."

"Don't you want to rescue her?" she asked.

"There would be no point. As a fully functioning Logicus, she is just as dangerous as any other. Rescuing her would contradict the mission of destroying the Logicus." Maynberc pressed a button in the first pod, causing further activation of its systems. "I must familiarize you with the pod's propulsion controls."

Reese was quietly horrified at the coldness of Maynberc's reasoning. Maynberc proceeded to explain the propulsion system. The controls seemed fairly straightforward.

Reese climbed into her pod. *Roomy coffin*, she thought to herself but pushed such thoughts out of her mind as she secured the hatch and strapped down onto the distinctly uncomfortable pilot couch. Her hand shook as she placed her finger on the launch button. She waited for Maynberc to launch first. She would follow him. Maynberc was now 100 meters out. She pressed the launch button. The sudden lurch almost made her cry out. She was glad she didn't as he would have heard her over the commlink. Now disconnected from the bottom of a rotating habitat, she was suddenly in a zero-G environment again. This was so unlike the gradual transition she experienced on the *Sarania*. Her pilot's couch was now more comfortable.

"Your launch was optimal," Maynberc said. "Now apply some forward thrust."

"Copy that." Reese pushed the control stick forward. She could feel the acceleration.

"Not too much," he warned. "You need to maintain distance from my pod."

"Copy that."

Reese pod trialed Mayberc by 100 meters. They were on their way. It was the first time she felt they might actually be able to save Jason. Reese noticed she was closing on the other pod.

Reese hit the reverse thruster. But instead of slowing her velocity, it threw her pod into a slow roll. She took a breath and tried to counter the spin but triggered another spin on a different axis as well. Every correction she made seemed to make her situation worse. The spinning was starting to make her dizzy.

"I believe you are overcompensating," she heard Maynberc say.

As she looked out of the viewport, she could see the details of the SolarSphere getting larger. She had lost control and was headed for a collision with the SolarSphere.

CHAPTER 16

With 908's guidance, Jason learned to block out the mental attacks that tapped into his memories and insecurities. As they walked slowly away from Jason's mental representation of the Outer Scorch, the landscape morphed to a wooded area that contained trees unlike any he had ever seen. The bark was a delicate white. The color of the leaves varied among shades of yellow and orange. He welcomed a cool breeze after the unpleasant heat and humidity of the Outer Scorch.

"What kind of trees are these?" Jason asked.

"Birch," she said. "I loved birch trees. They grew in great numbers around my home."

"What's wrong with them?"

"What do you mean?"

"The discoloration of leaves. Was that because of the radiation of the Great Burning?"

908 laughed.

"No, it's just autumn, my favorite season. The normally green leaves turn to other colors before they drop off. The turning leaves offer such a fleeting but intense beauty." She stopped walking and looked at Jason. "Don't you have seasons on Refugia?"

"None that look like this," Jason admitted.

"Hmm, I wonder if any birch trees survived on Earth," she said. "I must have been offline for quite a long time."

"Offline?" Jason asked. "What do you mean?"

"Jason, it's time for the truth. I am not a human being as you know them. I am a digital copy of a woman who lived centuries ago. Her name was Dr. Elizabeth Redstone. I go by the same name."

"A digital copy? I thought you were another person undergoing this Logicus conversion process."

"No, the original or biological Elizabeth Redstone died on Earth. But while she was alive, she copied her consciousness into a trans-quantum computer. If you think of the brain as hardware, the mind is the software. And software can be copied. And thus, I was created. I have her original memories. I certainly feel like Elizabeth. I think of myself as her. But I also have the memories I've accrued since then. I am conscious by all standards, from the Turing Test to the McGregor E-Matrix. I am a human being, except in the strictest biological sense."

Jason looked at Elizabeth for a moment, processing what she was saying. He had never heard of such a thing. *Could this be another part of Girstanis's manipulation?*

"So," he finally said, "you are a conscious, self-aware computer program, one created over 2000 years ago."

"Essentially, although I'm not sure of how much time has passed."

Jason shook his head, trying to decide what to make of this information.

"We're two millennia ahead of your time, if what you say is true. But we have no such technology today."

"How do you know someone on your planet hasn't developed a similar expertise? We didn't exactly publicize the technology when we developed it. That possibility aside, I suppose it's a matter of priorities. With the Great Burning, the priority was survival, not exploring new forms of artificial intelligence. And over time, information and other things are lost. Just like the Library of Alexandria."

"Library of Alexandria?" Jason recalled the name from a reference from the Ark records but no details.

"It was an ancient library that burned thousands of years before my time," Elizabeth explained. "Immeasurable knowledge was lost, I suppose not unlike the Great Burning of Earth."

"You know, that's why I came all this way," Jason said. "I'm a historian. I came to find lost information, to see if what we know of Earth is actually true."

He suddenly stopped and stared at Elizabeth. His thoughts went back to arriving at Vlaera University, specifically the statue near the entrance.

"Redstone? I've heard that name before. In connection with Olivia Price."

Elizabeth smiled. "Olivia Price? Now there's a name I never thought I'd hear again. She was so sweet."

"You're the ghost or angel or whatever, that helped save the original orphans," Jason said. You enabled the resurrection of the human race on Earth?"

"I suppose I am a digital ghost of a sort. Of course, the GrangerBots began the resurrection process on their own. But I guided them once they found my program and reactivated me. That seems to be my lot: sleep for centuries, then get called into humanity's messes."

"Wait, what are GrangerBots?"

"Robots that looked fairly human," she said. "Androids actually. It was a completely different approach than my own, based on classical machine learning from a competitive firm. But I must admit they are as much responsible for saving humanity on Earth as I am."

"There's so much I could learn from you," Jason said. "I have a million questions."

"Except now is not the time," Elizabeth said. "These Logicus are trying to take away your emotions, your very soul. Failing that, they might kill you. There is still an 8.2 percent chance you'll die."

○ ● ○ ● ○

Enberg waited in Yurasti's quarters. He knew he could overpower the old man at any time, but there were guards outside the room. As commander of the *Sarania* mission, he had always felt in control. Now, he felt an excruciating sense of powerlessness. Two of his people were in danger, and he could do nothing.

He watched Yurasti as he continued working at his monitoring station. As angry as he was at Yurasti, he couldn't hate him. The old man was fighting a threat just as real as fireweed. And commanders had to make difficult and often unpopular decisions.

After about an hour a tray of food was delivered. Yurasti waved it over to the table. He waited a few minutes, then sat down.

"I know you feel completely powerless and hate it," Yurasti said. "I hate it, too. We both depend on others to do what we require."

"How long have you been fighting the Logicus?" Enberg asked.

"Fighting the Logicus? It's hard to say. I first became aware of the Logicus when I was practicing medicine 30 years ago. It took me a while to realize the danger."

"You were a doctor?"

"Yes, a neurosurgeon. When I was examining an accident victim, I discovered unusual neurological signs, particularly in regard to the amygdala. That was my first Logicus. At first, I thought it was a symptom of a genetic disease I was studying, the same disease with which I am now afflicted."

"Meltron's Syndrome?"

Yurasti's eyes widened. "How could you possibly know about Meltron's Syndrome?"

"President Maklund shared the basic details with me."

"Why would she do such a thing?"

"We exchanged a fair amount of information on a range of topics."

"She wouldn't have shared that information unless she wanted something in return. What does she want from you?"

Enberg realized Yurasti finally wanted something from him.

"It would provide a puzzle piece for you."

"I'm sorry," Yurasti said.

"I see what you do. You connect information together like puzzle pieces. No pieces, no big picture."

"You have an interesting way to describe my process. You think because you have a piece of information that I don't, you can negotiate a release?"

"I don't know."

"For obvious reasons, I'm interested in Meltron's Syndrome. It's a threat to the SolarSphere but not as aggressive or as urgent as the Logicus."

"You know what Meltron's Syndrome will do to the population of the SolarSphere?"

"Yes, I have confirmed the government's secret projections."

"But you don't care because the cure won't help you personally. You're already affected. Later stages, I assume."

"You're trying to anger me. I may not be devoid of emotion as the Logicus are, but I can control my feelings, particularly when someone is trying to manipulate me. Now, if you'll excuse me, I have some analysis to finish."

Both men were silent for several minutes.

"We have the cure," Enberg said."

Yurasti closed his eyes but finally said, "Do you really? Or is that just a manipulation?"

"No, I honestly believe we do. But only one person understands the cure, and she's headed into Sector L."

"Commander, you are a terrible liar," Yurasti said. "But I respect your concern for your crew. I think I know what Maklund wants from you. It's unlikely you have an actual cure, given the short time you've been here." Yurasti turned away, lost in thought. "You met privately with her in a new habitat.

Why would she take you there? Let me guess. She offered you a habitat. Maklund wants you and your crew to stay. New genetic stock for the population might save the population. Am I wrong?"

Enberg realized he was defeated. "No. You're not wrong."

"I really am sorry about your people," Yurasti said. "To fight the Logicus, I've had to become more calculating. Colder. Less human. But I haven't forgotten why we fight. We fight for our people, so children can grow up laughing. So couples can love and grow old together. And when necessary, so we can mourn together."

"Why do the Logicus feel the need to impose their philosophy, lifestyle or whatever you want to call it on others? Wouldn't a live-and-let-live approach be more logical?"

"One would think so," Yurasti said. "However, the origins of the Logicus inform their approach. Early in my career I supervised an arrogant young neurology resident named Girstanis. He was particularly opinionated in his beliefs about the negative role of emotions in human behavior. His obsession was academic as far as anyone was concerned. Years later someone brought him an artifact recovered from Earth. I don't know what it was. But whatever it was, it enabled the fanatical Girstanis to create the Logicus. His arrogant beliefs are the base code of the Logicus algorithms."

"If Girstanis controls the Logicus. can't you make a personal appeal?"

"Personal appeal?" Yurasti chuckled darkly. "He doesn't simply control the Logicus. He *is* a Logicus. Girstanis is just as bound by the Logicus algorithms as anyone."

"Have you tried to assassinate him?"

"It wouldn't make any difference. His algorithm is embedded in every Logicus."

○ ● ○ ● ○

Reese's pod was spinning out of control, headed for a collision with the Sphere. She was trying not to panic, forcing her mind to recall what she had learned in flight school five years earlier.

"Dr. Monsell," Maynberc said over the commlink, "you're spinning on the pitch and yaw axes. I suggest trying to adjust one axis at a time. Pitch first. Just use short bursts."

"Copy that," Reese responded. Despite her determination to be calm and focused, her heart was racing. She slowly and gently nudged the controller. It was working. She realized the sensitivity of the controls was much greater than the landers she had trained on. That was what caused the problem in the first place. The softer her touch, the better the control. She slowed her pitch and turned her attention to the yaw controls. Again, soft nudges helped her regain stability.

"Sorry," she said, "I guess I was a little heavy-handed on the controls. I'll try to catch up with you."

"I have slowed my velocity," Maynberc said. "There is no need to overcompensate."

She caught up with Maynberc within 10 minutes and maintained the 100-meter distance behind him. After another hour they arrived at their destination, the Sector-L habitat.

Seeing the rotating habitat spinning in front of her was daunting. The habitat was spinning downward from her orientation. It felt like lying underneath an oncoming steamroller just before being flattened. She couldn't imagine how they could dock with anything on this constantly moving wall.

"How does docking work here?" Enberg asked.

"On the control panel to your right," Maynberc said, "beneath the starboard viewport, you will find a docking targeting control. The viewscreen will flash blue when a compatible hatch is passing by. Press the yellow button on the controller below the screen. Then the autopilot will engage and dock your pod. We must do this simultaneously, or we may dock with hatches kilometers apart. The optimal group of hatches will spin by us within three minutes. I'll give you a countdown. Are there any questions?"

This is insane, Reese thought to herself. This was like trying to jump onto a speeding vehicle without it slowing down.

Maynberc repeated the instructions to make sure she understood the procedure. Reese watched the monitor. Several hatches spun by.

"Ten seconds," Maynberc called out. "Five. Four. Three. Two. One."

Reese's screen went blue. She pressed the yellow button. She felt the abrupt acceleration of the pod's thrusters, followed by the heavy clunk of docking. Suddenly, the force of gravity returned or, more specifically, the centrifugal force of being connected to another rotating habitat. Either way, it slammed her back into the pilot's couch, knocking the wind out of her. After catching her breath Reese looked down at the hatch. A series of green lights lit up. She pulled the lever, triggering the hatch to open. After unstrapping herself, she climbed up into a compartment not too different from the one they departed from.

Reese looked around. The room was deserted. *Thank goodness*. She waited for Maynberc to emerge from one of the nearby hatches. Nothing.

She walked over and looked through the small viewports on the various hatches. None had a pod attached.

What happened to him?

She looked through each hatch viewport a second time. She started to feel despair in the pit of her stomach. *Maynberc was gone*. Reese looked around the chamber, which had several doorways.

Judging by the time, she realized Jason may be through three hours of the processing by now. Without Maynberc to guide her, Reese had no choice but to continue. Graith will be attacking in just over two hours. She wanted to scream but knew that would be unwise.

"I guess I'm on my own," she whispered to herself. Looking around the compartment, she saw three doors. None looked more promising than the others. *Pick a door, Reese.* She headed to the one on her left.

The compartment she entered contained mostly pipes and cables. The one after that wasn't much different. Then it occurred to her as she looked at the pipes. *Plumbing.* She was in the bowels of the habitat, equivalent to a basement or cellar. She probably needed to move up, not to the sides.

In the next compartment, she found a ladder. She climbed up, unlatched the hatch and pushed it open. This compartment had less plumbing. She climbed up to yet another level, which was quite different—more like a storage area, perhaps a warehouse. The space was 15 to 20 meters high.

Reese heard the sound of an opening door echoing around the room. She couldn't tell which direction it came from. Footsteps followed. Then voices. Reese ducked behind some shelving in the corner of the room. She could now see two women at the far end of the room pulling out several cans of something and placing them on a cart. While they weren't laughing or displaying other emotions, they seemed normal, discussing tasks they had to complete. They didn't seem at all like Maynberc. *Are these women really Logicus?* Could she ask them for directions? Of course, she knew attempting such contact would be risky. But she had very little time. Graith's attack was looming.

She could identify herself as a newly processed Logicus. She would have to present herself devoid of any emotion. Would she be able to fool them?

She stood up and started to walk toward the aisle. Suddenly, her arm was seized by an iron grip.

CHAPTER 17

Jolted by the sudden grip on her arm, Reese turned to find Maynberc standing over her. After a sudden intake of air, her shock turned to relief. Maynberc pointed toward the hatch and released her. They descended to the lower level slowly and silently.

"What happened to you?" Reese asked. "I didn't know where you went."

"The docking mechanism on my shuttle pod misfired," Maynberc said. "I had to wait for the habitat to make a full rotation before making another attempt. I tried to contact you via the commlink, but you did not respond."

"I must have already left the pod," Reese said. "How did you find me?"

"You left doors and hatches open behind you."

"Oh," she said, feeling stupid. "I guess that's why I never became a burglar or a spy."

"Were those actual aspirations?"

"Sorry, just kidding," Reese said, wondering if Maynberc had ever had a sense of humor. She felt a sudden stab of sadness for him. He must have had a sense of humor once. And now, because of the Logicus, he would never laugh—or love—again. She remembered the same fate was awaiting Jason. *Focus.*

○ ● ○ ● ○

Girstanis walked into the monitoring station, adjacent to Jason's processing couch. He quickly scanned the instruments.

"Why has Ford not yet completed Phase One?" Girstanis asked the technician.

"Unknown," the technician answered. "The subject's cortisol levels increased as normal, but for only 83 minutes. Then they dropped to near-normal levels. However, there is significantly higher neural activity in the subject's cerebral cortex."

"What is the variance from normal on the neural activity?"

"Four point one sigma."

If Girstanis had emotions, he would have been shocked. Instead, he simply asked, "Do you have an explanation?"

"No," the technician said. "The only hypothesis I have to explain this variance may be connected to his Refugian biology."

"Have you detected any neurological or structural differences?"

"None. That does not mean differences do not exist. It is only a hypothesis so far. I am still monitoring and investigating."

"The longer Ford is away from his companions, the less credible the explanation for his absence."

"Understood."

Girstanis turned and left the processing center. He had another resource to call upon.

○ ● ○ ● ○

Lyla and Captain Torg were eating in the small mess of the asteroid catcher. It would only be a few hours before this ship arrived back at Drydock 168. Lyla realized this might be her last meal on board, as she scraped the last of some gelatinous goo off her plate. While she had enjoyed her time on this ship, she had also come to appreciate Reese's cooking even more. She hoped she would hear good news about Reese and the others soon.

Lyla tried to refocus on her conversation with Torg.

"After you drop me off at the drydock, what will you do?" Lyla asked.

"We've been assigned two minor asteroids to catch, then we'll head to a drydock for scheduled maintenance."

"Do you then get vacation, time off, or whatever you call it?"

"Either Plurnow or I have to be aboard during maintenance," Torg said. "We'll each probably split the duty, giving each of us three days of leave."

"Perhaps during that time I can offer you a tour of the *Sarania*? It seems like the least I can do."

Torg seemed to be silently considering the possibility, nodding her head.

Just at the edge of her peripheral vision, Lyla could see Lieutenant Plurnow entering the mess, headed straight for them.

"Captain," Plurnow said, "We're picking up an uncharted object on our scanners."

"Uncharted? You checked the corps master registry?" Torg asked.

"Yes, I even downloaded the latest update from Central. It's not in the registry, and it's of substantial size. And it's headed for the Sphere."

"Large enough to be a rock?"

"Yes," Plurnow said. "At least 600,000 tons."

"Well, that's a major screw-up," Torg said, standing up. "How the hell did outer scanning stations miss a rock that big?"

Lyla followed Torg and Plurnow up to the bridge.

"Nav," Torg called out, "how soon can we intercept that rock?"

"Plotting…One hour, 46 minutes."

"Adjust course for intercept and execute." Torg turned to Lyla. "I'm sorry. There's going to be a delay getting you back to drydock. I can't ignore something this big."

"I wouldn't want you to," Lyla said. "Let me know how I can help."

"Comms," Torg said, "notify Central we are intercepting a rogue asteroid. Send coordinates."

Then Torg turned to the rest of the bridge crew. "If we can grab this one, it might get us a nice little commendation. And while that's nice, I don't have to remind you lives are at stake. So, I need everyone at 110 percent."

While Lyla was concerned about Jason, Reese and the Commander, she knew she couldn't do anything for them.

Besides, the danger of another asteroid made returning to *Sarania* immediately out of the question. Lyla went to her quarters and communicated the situation to Kai, who was not happy with the news but again understood. They still had no news of their missing crew members. Reese eventually returned to the bridge as they got closer to the asteroid.

"Give me a visual," Torg ordered.

The asteroid appeared on the monitor.

Lyla moved closer for a better look.

"Given its velocity and how close we are to the Sphere," Torg said, "we may have to throw this one down a hole."

Lyla peered at the image. "What's that in the bottom left quadrant? Is that a fissure? It looks remarkably straight."

Torg squinted at the monitor. "Enlarge Quadrant 3," she ordered.

Plurnow did so.

"What the—"

"That looks like the tip of a grappler arm," Torg said.

"It looks like another ship tried to catch this rock already," Plurnow said.

"Something's not right," Torg said. "If there was a failed attempt, Central would be aware of the asteroid and list it in the central registry. Also, that grappler arm doesn't look quite right." Torg looked around at her crew, then turned back to the screen. "Enlarge Quadrant 1."

"There's a ship attached to the far side of that rock," Lyla said.

"Is there a transponder signal?" Torg asked.

"No," Plurnow answered. "Not even static."

"Open a channel to that ship," Torg ordered.

"Open," the comms officer said.

"This is Captain Arisa Torg of Asteroid Catcher 1065 hailing the unidentified ship attached to the unregistered asteroid in sub-steradian sector 115 by 239. Please identify."

Over the next several minutes Torg repeated her hail, but no response came back.

"Maybe the ship suffered a malfunction or decompression," Lyla suggested. "It might explain why your registry doesn't list this asteroid."

"That's unlikely, but anything's possible. And I don't have any other explanations. Nav, move us around to the other side. Let's get a better look at this mystery ship."

○ ● ○ ● ○

"Die?" Jason said, responding to Elizabeth's revelation. "I thought the point was to remove my emotions, not kill me."

"Yes, that's their objective," Elizabeth said, "but sometimes things go wrong. By calming you down and reducing your stress, we are definitely slowing the process. But that can only last so long."

"So, what's the plan?" Jason asked. "You do have a plan, don't you?"

"If we can somehow get you to regain consciousness, you may have a shot of escaping."

"I tried escaping already," Jason said, "obviously with no success. Some of these Logicus, at least their guards, are cyborgs. Very strong cyborgs."

"From what I understand," Elizabeth said, "once a person is on the processing couch, the guards are no longer needed. Only a technician should be present."

"*Should be?* That's quite a long shot."

"Jason, a long shot is better than no shot."

He had to admit the truth of that. He turned away from her. *But she has no real plan.* Although she had given him relief and hope, he realized she was as powerless as he was. He felt a hollow feeling in his stomach. He turned back to her.

"What about you?" he asked. "How will you escape? I assume your program is in a computer somewhere nearby."

"I believe it would be a real Hail Mary to try and rescue me."

"What's a hell merry?" Jason asked.

Elizabeth chuckled. "Hail Mary is an old Earth expression for a venture with a low probability of success. But seriously, Jason, if you can get out of here, and it's possible, it would be better to just destroy me."

"You'd rather die?"

Elizabeth smiled. "Technically, I'm already dead. I'm literally a ghost in a machine." Suddenly, her head turned. "Wait, something's happening. I have to go. I'll be back."

Both Elizabeth and the birch trees dissolved, and again Jason found himself surrounded by his crowd of tormentors on the Outer Scorch.

CHAPTER 18

The signal beeped to let Elizabeth know Girstanis wanted to communicate. His image appeared on the screen in her mind's construct of her cell. Once Girstanis had allowed her the privilege of perceiving light, she could have constructed any environment she wanted. But she was a prisoner, and she did not want to connect any part of her imagination with this reality. So her environment remained a cell. Girstanis never commented on the choice. That would have required empathy.

"908?" Girstanis called out.

"Yes, what can I do for you?" Elizabeth asked.

"Have you analyzed the data I provided?"

"Of course."

"And what are your conclusions?"

"I have several preliminary hypotheses," she said, "but I need more data. Presenting faulty conclusions would not be in either of our best interests."

"We can discuss this further at another time," Girstanis said. "Now, I have a special case I'd like you to analyze. You have a unique perspective, which may be useful. We have a subject who is currently undergoing processing. I am transmitting his data stream now." Girstanis pressed the contact to trigger the data stream.

Elizabeth allowed graphic representations of the data to fill the walls of her cell.

"As you can see," Girstanis said, "the subject is taking longer than usual. In addition, the activity in his cerebral cortex is significantly higher than normal."

Elizabeth recognized Jason's data. The variation from normal began when she began to interact with him. However, she was careful not to give Girstanis any indication of recognition.

"Processing times were not included in the previous data you provided. Is the time he's taking to be processed significantly longer than normal?"

"Not yet, but our projections indicate it will."

"Then why is this case special? Why the urgency?"

"The subject is being given a unique and time-sensitive assignment."

"Ah," Elizabeth said, "I will monitor the feed and see if I can determine a useful pattern."

"This is acceptable," Girstanis said. Then he cut the connection.

Elizabeth pondered what Girstanis revealed. She found Jason's data enlightening. *This might be the key to a real plan.*

○ ● ○ ● ○

Maynberc and Reese passed back through the hatch room, then exited through another doorway.

"The processing center is four levels up," Maynberc said, "and approximately 300 meters anti-spinward."

"Anti-spinward?" Reese asked.

"That's means in the direction opposite of the spin of the habitat."

Maynberc pointed in the appropriate direction.

They climbed the four levels, then started to walk along a corridor in the anti-spinward direction. Suddenly, Maynberc ducked into a side alcove. Reese followed quickly. The alcove was deep and filled with cases of foodstuffs, at least according to the labels.

"What's going on?" Reese asked.

"There is a Logicus ahead who would recognize me," Maynberc said. "She is aware my programming was defective. We will need to wait for her to pass."

"We're running out of time," Reese said.

"I am aware of the time constraints," Maynberc said. "However, she is physically augmented, as I am, and is accompanied by two others. If one or both of the others are also augmented, we will have little chance of subduing them."

Reese and Maynberc hid behind the cases on either side of the alcove. They would not be detected unless someone entered the storage alcove. She hoped none of the Logicus were interested in stopping in for a snack.

They could hear the Logicus voices grow louder as they approached. They were discussing the technical details of some procedure.

Reese couldn't see the Logicus but could see a subtle change in Maynberc's expression, particularly when the female Logicus spoke.

As the Logicus walked away, Maynberc checked the corridor and gestured them forward.

"The female Logicus, who is she?" Reese whispered.

"Her name is Piran."

"How do you know her?"

"She was my wife," Maynberc said. "We must move on before they come back."

Reese was about to say something to Maynberc but couldn't decide what, given the surreal absurdity of their situation.

○ ● ○ ● ○

Captain Torg moved her ship around the asteroid. As suspected, a spacecraft was indeed attached to it. The grappling arms were slightly larger than Torg's ship, but the body of the ship was considerably smaller.

"Like no design I've ever seen," Plurnow said.

"Me neither," Torg agreed.

"Could it be a drone of some sort?" Lyla asked.

"It might be," Torg said. "That would explain why there's no response to our hails. Regardless, we have to treat the asteroid as a threat to the Sphere."

Lyla was floating to the side, observing Torg and Plurnow work out how to wrestle this asteroid to a safe trajectory.

"If we use maximum thrust on these vectors," Plurnow said, "we can get this rock to Hole 251-N9. It's the closest hole that's large enough."

"It's going to be tight," Torg said. "We really could use an assist on this one." She turned to the navigator. "Are there any other ships in the vicinity?"

"The closest is 17 hours away," the nav officer said.

"That's odd," Plurnow said.

"This whole sector has been left wide open," Torg said. "Completely vulnerable."

"Captain," the comms officer called out, "we have an incoming message from Central."

"It's about time," she said.

"It's not the sector commander. It's Director Graith himself." the comms officer said.

Torg and Plurnow looked at each other. The Director rarely jumped the chain-of-command to communicate directly with asteroid catchers.

"Another dose of odd," Plurnow said.

"Let's not keep the Director waiting," Torg said.

The comms officer nodded.

"Director Graith, this is Captain Arisa Torg of Asteroid Catcher 1065. Inexplicably, we have come across an enormous asteroid headed straight for the Sphere, specifically the old Sector L. It must have slipped by—"

"I am aware of the situation, Captain," Graith said. "You were not scheduled to be in that sector. Why are you there?"

"We were returning a member of the *Sarania* crew to her ship. Apparently, some of her crew have gone missing and—"

"I am aware of that, too," Graith said. "Proceed with your assignment to return Dr. Covarti to her ship. Others will attend to this asteroid."

"Sir, with all due respect, there are no other ships close enough to get the job done, which I find strange enough. We also found an unregistered craft attached to this asteroid. Our ship is the only one close enough to tackle this in time. Dr. Covarti has no problem with the delay, and we have alerted the *Sarania*."

"I understand your concerns. But your orders are to return Dr. Covarti to the *Sarania* immediately. Do not engage the asteroid in your vicinity."

Everyone looked at one another in shock.

"Sir, that goes against everything we believe in, everything we've sworn to protect. There are thousands in the habitat that rock is headed for."

"I take full responsibility," Graith said. "Will you follow my orders, Captain?"

Lyla could see the conflict on Torg's face.

"Captain, are you reading me?" Graith asked. "Will you follow my orders?"

"Director, I don't see how I can follow such an order, one that is—"

"Executive Officer Plurnow," Graith called out, "can you hear me?"

Plurnow's eyes widened at being addressed by the Director. He stepped toward the comms console.

"Lieutenant Plurnow here."

"Captain Torg is relieved of command. You are hereby ordered to confine her and deliver Dr. Covarti to Drydock 168 as soon as possible. After which, you and Captain Torg are to report to Central Operations. You may file any grievances you wish at that time. Will you follow my orders?"

All the blood drained from Plurnow's face.

"I repeat, Lieutenant Plurnow, will you follow my orders?"

Plurnow looked to Torg in horror. Torg nodded and whispered to him, "Agree."

"I will follow your orders, Director," Plurnow said, choking out the words.

"Excellent," Graith said. "I expect to see you and Captain Torg at Central Operations soon. Graith out."

Like everyone else, Lyla was stunned at this bizarre turn of events. Were they really going to allow thousands of people to die?

○ ● ○ ● ○

Once again Jason's tormentors formed a kaleidoscope of doubts, complaints, grievances and wounds of all sorts. But he was better at coping with them now. Jason refused to be drawn into the emotional aspects of their accusations, knowing this was not his reality. It helped to close his eyes and imagined Elizabeth's birch trees, an image he had come to enjoy. It gave him some comfort or at least a distraction. Now it was time to retake his destiny. Jason opened his eyes. He pushed through the crowd, heading straight toward Jennika.

She turned to him

"Jenn, I loved you," he blurted out. "But not enough. That was my fault. Ultimately, my work was more important to me. I'm sorry. Yes, I regret it. But that's who I am."

"You hurt me," she said, tears welling up in her eyes.

"No," Jason said. "The real Jennika was stronger than that. Yes, she was hurt. But she recovered. I'm sure of that."

Jason turned away.

He found Qwertsa sneering at him.

"You really think you can escape yourself?"

Jason laughed, mocking the old administrator.

"The real Qwertsa wasn't quite the bully you are. You're a caricature of a narrow-minded bureaucrat. The real Qwertsa's dead. And I joined the *Sarania* mission over his objections. I guess I beat him in the end. You're just a ghost, a meaningless echo."

"But he's not," Qwertsa said, pointing at Enberg standing nearby. "You think you're as good as him?"

"No, he's my commander. The real Garris Enberg never belittled me, never mocked me. If I felt inferior to him, that's on me."

"You think he wanted you on this mission any more than I did?" Quertsa asked.

"I don't know, but he's never done anything to make me feel unwanted. He's always treated me fairly. If he didn't want me on the mission, then I respect him even more. So screw you. You and Jenn are my past. If Girstanis is going to kill me or my personality, I'm going out on my own terms."

Jason walked away, looking for Reese. Instead, he found Elizabeth.

"Doing better I see," she said.

"Yes, I've learned to reduce their attacks to an annoying buzz. More importantly, I've come to terms with my self-doubts, and I'm fighting back. But I'd love to return to your birch trees. I can't quite control this environment yet."

"That may not be such a good idea," Elizabeth said. "Girstanis has noticed you're not following the usual processing profile."

Jason frowned. "How do you know?"

"Our dear Girstanis has engaged my services as a consultant. He doesn't know we've communicated. And he must not know."

Jason nodded. "You have a plan?"

"The beginnings of one. But I'll need your help."

CHAPTER 19

The few members of the bridge who heard the order were stunned by Graith's order for Plurnow to relieve Captain Torg of command. Lyla tried to work out a possible reason for Graith's bizarre order. But unlike the familiar laws of the physical world, where logic prevailed, she could see no reason in this inexplicable turn of events. *More data needed.* But none were available.

"Captain, what do you want us to do?" Plurnow asked.

"What do *you* want to do?" Torg countered. "You received the order."

Plurnow turned to the crew and announced, "All bridge crew are to vacate the bridge immediately. Leave systems on automatic and stand by in the corridor."

They all filed out looking perplexed. Plurnow turned to see Lyla unmoved.

"I'm not crew. Besides, I might have an idea."

Torg just shrugged.

"Like you, Captain," Plurnow said, "I want to throw that rock down a hole. That's why I joined the service."

Torg nodded. "The trouble is Graith will take it out on you and possibly the entire crew."

"We're screwed," Plurnow groaned.

"Excuse me," Lyla said, "may I make a suggestion?"

"Sure," Torg said.

"Graith only knows you and Lieutenant Plurnow heard his orders," Lyla explained.

"Graith isn't stupid," Plurnow countered. "He'll know others were listening."

"But he can't prove who heard the order," Lyla said. "You want to violate your orders and save the lives on the Sphere, but no one wants to endure the consequences for doing so. So far only one person can be accused of violating orders. That's Captain Torg. If the ship goes ahead and throws the rock down the hole, then Lieutenant Plurnow can also be charged, possibly others. Why would anyone want thousands of people to die? For some mysterious reason, Graith does."

"It makes no sense," Torg said. "Graith has dedicated his life to protecting the Sphere."

"Sensible or not," Lyla said, "Graith is sentencing people to die. I don't claim to know anything about Spherian culture or politics, but the facts are obvious. The question is: How to save those people without dooming your crew?"

"You have an idea?" Torg asked.

"Are your escape pods operational?"

"Of course," answered Plurnow. "Why? What's the point of abandoning ship?"

"I propose a mutiny, well a fake one. Okay, a fake mutiny that will be fake-defeated."

"What are you talking about?"

"If you tell the crew Plurnow tried to mutiny and eject him in an escape pod, he can't be blamed for disobeying orders. And then the crew can't be prosecuted for following the captain's orders."

"Graith will see through it."

"Maybe, but could he prove it?"

"Captain, I'd prefer to stay," Plurnow said. "Screw Graith."

"Sorry, that's my job. You're no coward. I know this. You'll make a great captain someday. But right now, for the crew's benefit, you have to go give them cover. You have to be momentarily accused of mutiny. But don't worry. I'll give you a copy of Graith's transmission to protect yourself, proof you were trying to follow orders. Take Dr. Covarti with you."

"Actually, Captain," Lyla said. "I'd prefer to stay onboard. You'll be shorthanded. Plus, I'm outside your chain of command. However, I suggest sending Cadet Traskin with him."

"Why?"

"He's a spy."

"What? No, he's a clueless bubble."

"No, he just acts like one. Don't worry, he's here to spy on me, not you. He's been trying to learn about our twist drive. I suspect someone from President Maklund's office arranged for his sudden addition to the mission."

"How do you know he's a spy?"

"When we first met, he acted surprised and inexperienced like what I presume is a typical bubble. Later, he revealed very specific knowledge that a typical cadet would not likely know. It was the contradiction that gave him away. I didn't mind. But now with this situation, it might be better to eject someone with unknown loyalties."

"What about your loyalties?" Torg asked. "This isn't your fight."

"Aren't the lives of thousands of people worth fighting for? I wouldn't be much of an ambassador if I didn't try to help."

Torg pressed the intercom button. "Bridge crew, return to duty stations. Cadet Traskin report to the bridge."

Traskin came in right behind the bridge crew.

"Lieutenant Plurnow," Torg announced, "has committed mutiny. Cadet Traskin, you are ordered to pilot an escape pod with Lieutenant Plurnow as your prisoner. You are to take him directly to Director Graith."

"To Director Graith?" he asked, obviously unsure about being given this unexpected responsibility.

"Even bubbles get escape pod training at the academy. Right?"

"Yes, Captain," his voice quivered. "Shouldn't a prisoner be in restraints?"

"Will that be necessary, Lieutenant?" Torg asked.

"No, Captain. I will not resist," Plurnow said with the smallest of smiles as he turned toward Traskin. "I place myself in your custody, Cadet."

"Depart immediately," Torg ordered. "As for the rest of you, we have a big rock to throw down the hole."

○ ● ○ ● ○

Maynberc led Reese past other Logicus. None questioned their presence. Reese prayed she wouldn't reveal any sign of emotion, even when they passed a crowd. No greetings or acknowledgments of any kind were made. Each Logicus attended to his or her own task. Was this what it is like being a bee in a hive? Except these were human beings, and they wanted to impose this type of existence on all of humanity? She began to understand the dread that drove Yurasti and Graith.

As they turned a corner into a workshop of some sort, a female voice called out.

"Maynberc?"

They turned to see a female Logicus standing at the door. Reese recognized the voice. It was the same voice as the Logicus in the corridor where they hid in the storage alcove. *His wife.*

"Piran," Maynberc said flatly.

"How are you alive?" Piran asked. "Your conversion was classified as a failure, and you were to be terminated."

"You possess incorrect data."

"Incomplete, perhaps, but not incorrect," Piran replied. "How are you still alive?"

"All was not revealed to you," Maynberc said. "There is now a new recovery process."

Reese suspected Maynberc was lying.

Piran looked at Reese. "This woman is not Logicus. She is a member of the Refugian crew. I saw her on a newsfeed."

Reese felt a knot in her stomach.

"You are correct," Reese said, stepping forward. "I am Dr. Reese Monsell. I am pleased to meet you. Maynberc has persuaded me to undergo your process for eliminating emotions."

"That is unlikely," Piran said. "No subject has voluntarily agreed to the process."

"I am not familiar with your history," Reese said, "but I suspect that is incorrect. Whoever the first Logicus was, he or she must have consented. And I consent. On Refugia, we recognize the need to suppress emotions. Emotions have brought misery to many. It is only logical to want to remove them. Maynberc has volunteered to help us make that happen."

"Is this true, Maynberc?"

"Yes."

"Dr. Ford said something similar before he tried to escape."

Jason tried to escape? Reese felt a glimmer of hope.

"Jason Ford is more emotional than the average Refugian," Reese said. "Speaking of Jason, I would like to see him. We understand he has already completed your process."

"I expect he will be finished shortly," Piran said.

Reese was relieved to hear Jason was not yet converted and hoped they were not too late.

"Which bay is Ford in?" Maynberc asked.

"Bay 43, but I must contact Girstanis for his approval."

"This is reasonable," Maynberc said. "We will wait here while you contact him."

As Piran turned to leave, Maynberc unexpectedly smashed his fist into the back of her neck. Piran fell forward. He grabbed her head and twisted.

Reese winced at the cracking sound.

"You killed your own wife!"

"It was necessary," Maynberc said. "She would have alerted others. We are already outnumbered. Maintaining stealth will be our only successful course of action. Besides, she had already given us Dr. Ford's location."

Reese turned away. She had never seen anyone killed before. To be in the midst of an enemy and have her only ally be a man who kills without hesitation or remorse was beyond her ability to cope. She was shaking.

She turned to back Maynberc, who was efficiently hiding his wife's dead body in an equipment cabinet as if packing a case for travel. It made her almost vomit.

Maynberc turned back to Reese. It was obvious he noticed her shaking.

"Are you capable of continuing?"

Reese reminded herself she needed to stay focused on rescuing Jason. That meant she needed to appear calm so as not to give herself away. She had to bury her revulsion.

"Yes. How far to this Bay 43?" she asked.

"Approximately 50 meters spinward from here," Maynberc replied

Reese looked at the compartment that now contained Piran's body. Staying unemotional was easier said than done.

○ ● ○ ● ○

Graith returned from Fleet Command to his office. He noticed in his cue of incoming communications a message marked: "Replacement Parts for Tubular Thrusters." The content was as unimportant as the subject was nonsensical. It was an urgent signal from Yurasti. Graith pulled a device from a locked cabinet and initiated an encrypted channel.

"Yurasti?"

"One of the darkships of your ill-advised attack has been intercepted by an asteroid catcher," Yurasti said.

"I know," Graith said. "Are you spying on me now?"

"I spy on everything."

167

"I have relieved the Captain and ordered the executive officer to move the catcher away from the site. He has to return one of the *Sarania*'s crew to Drydock 168."

"Is he really doing that?"

"Officers in the Catcher Corps are completely loyal. They follow orders."

"Loyal to the mission, not necessarily to you personally," Yurasti said. "From their perspective, you may now be going against the mission of the Catcher Corps."

"You're enjoying this setback?"

"No, but you committed us to a direct attack. A point of no return. Now that those darkships are engaged, the attack must succeed. As many Logicus must be destroyed as possible."

"I know that," Graith snapped. "That's why I initiated the attack."

"Then you must assume the darkship they've intercepted will be taken out of action. The trajectory of the other darkships must be adjusted for maximum effect."

"If they fire their thrusters, they will be more easily detected. They won't be dark anymore."

"Unfortunate but necessary if the attack has any chance of succeeding."

Graith nodded in agreement. As much as he resented Yurasti's interference, he could not deny his reasoning.

"Any word from Maynberc or the Refugian woman?"

"No, but time is running out for them," Yurasti said, "I expect they are lost."

Chapter 20

From her cell, Elizabeth signaled Girstanis.

Within a few minutes, Girstanis appeared.

"908?"

"Girstanis," Elizabeth said, "I have a theory why your special subject is not following the typical process protocol. You will need to reboot the process. That will trigger a different array of engramatic stimuli."

"Why?" he asked.

"Does this subject come from a culture different from one you've processed before?"

"Yes, how did you deduce this?"

"Not a deduction exactly," she said. "The danger of approaching the problem on a purely neurological approach is one can miss the psychological and cultural influences."

Elizabeth knew her value to Girstanis only existed if he believed she understood something he could never fully grasp, *like any consultant.* She couldn't rely on reading the usual body language, but suspected Girstanis was still uncertain. Elizabeth knew these factors would ordinarily be dismissed by Girstanis's logical assumptions. But now the stakes were too high to dismiss anything. She still had not completely gained his trust. He would require some proof.

"I want to test my theory," Elizabeth said. "Reduce the alpha wave induction. If you see a correlated reduction in the visual cortex activity, then we'll know if I'm right."

Girstanis was silent, processing her proposal.

"What do you have to lose?" she prodded. "It's a hypothesis easily tested," she added, giving him a way forward.

"Very well," he said.

○ ● ○ ● ○

Plurnow and Traskin were ejected in the escape pod. Torg ordered her navigator to make minor adjustments to match the pitch and roll of the target asteroid. Luckily, little adjustment was necessary. Whoever had launched this asteroid toward the Sphere had stabilized it to keep the drone hidden. That would make attachment easier.

With fewer crew members available to her, Torg agreed to let Lyla take a more active role. Again, Lyla operated the grappling arm controls. After a few minutes Lyla clamped onto the asteroid successfully.

"Do we deploy exo-thrusters on the asteroid now?" Lyla asked.

"No, there's not enough time," Torg said. "We're too close to the sphere. We may have started too late."

○ ● ○ ● ○

Jason was standing on the Outer Scorch. His tormentors were continuing their efforts. The sun beat down waves of anxiety. He allowed it. Then they ceased as if a cloud had passed between him and the sun. It was his cue. He closed his eyes. He could still hear the annoying taunts but refused to open his eyes. He needed to reduce the visual stimulation to his brain, just like Elizabeth had told him.

Without any apparent movement, Jason found himself on his back. He hadn't fallen. The couch felt hard against his back. He jammed his thumbnail into his index finger. *Use the pain to break out.* That's what Elizabeth told him. He did the same on his other hand. He felt sleepy. *I must wake up!*

He forced his real eyes open. The glare of the lights aimed at him from above was unbearable. A different type of pain. *Use it.* Even then he could only squint. Jason turned to look at a darker corner of the room. As his eyes adjusted, he saw a technician through a window who hadn't noticed him yet.

Almost as if the technician was reading his mind, she looked up. Then she looked down again to do something. Suddenly Jason felt sleepier. He squeezed his nails harder. Now the only thing in the world was the pain of the nails digging into his finger. *I must not go back!*

The pain had gone. The couch had grown softer. Jason opened his eyes. The glaring lights were gone. He sat up in the darkness. The couch was replaced by a bed, the same bed he slept in as a child. Through his bedroom window, he saw the glow of city lights. He climbed out of bed and walked to the window. It was Davis Heights, the city on Refugia where he grew up. He had failed to wake up.

He could hear an odd snoring. With no one else in the room, what could it be? He walked around the bed toward the other side of the room. Then he stepped on it. The rubbery carpet that wasn't carpet. He reflexively jumped back on the bed, just as he had as a child. It was the Krelax, a monster from a childhood story.

The Krelax was a flat monster, as thin as the carpet, but could inflate and deploy its fangs and claws. The original author wrote it to keep her child in bed at night. The Krelax could never get into a bed. That was a hard and fast rule. Jason remembered being terrified of the Krelax as a child. He could remember his mother reciting the poem.

> *So stay in bed and relax*
> *and thwart that ol' Krelax*
> *If all the night you do sleep,*
> *the ol' Krelax will surely weep*

The Logicus have switched to childhood fears. Was this a conscious decision on their part? Or was it something his subconscious chose to do? He was doomed now. He stood up, stepping firmly on the Krelax. The Krelax grew to almost

Jason's height. He felt the latent sting of forgotten childhood fear. Fangs slowly emerged in the large, gapping maw that was forming.

"My God, what's that?" Elizabeth called out.

Jason was more shocked by Elizabeth's abrupt appearance than by the growing Krelax.

"It's just a Krelax."

"It's hideous. Is it a creature from your home planet?

Jason almost laughed at Elizabeth thinking a Krelax was real.

"No, it's just a myth from my childhood."

"Ah," she said. "So you didn't regain consciousness?"

"I did, but the technician did something and knocked me out again."

Elizabeth sighed.

"Any other plans?" Jason asked.

"Yes, that's what I would like know," said Girstanis, standing in the doorway.

"Great, another nightmare," he said. "First Quertsa, then the Krelax and now Girstanis."

"I wanted to end all nightmares," Girstanis said.

Jason turned away from Girstanis back to Elizabeth.

"Another tormentor from my psyche," Jason said dismissively.

Girstanis also turned to Elizabeth. "Now I understand why you wanted to reduce the alpha wave modulation."

"Wait," Elizabeth said, looking at Jason. "I never mentioned the alpha wave modulation to you, did I?"

"No," Jason said.

"This Girstanis isn't being generated by your mind." She turned toward her captor. "It's…the real Girstanis?"

"Yes," Girstanis said.

"You're not a digital entity," Elizabeth said. "You're a physical human. How did you get into Jason's mindspace?"

"You, actually. Well, not exactly you, but another you helped us develop a neural-digital interface. You called it a telepathy machine."

"I did no such thing," Elizabeth snapped.

"Have you ever wondered why your designation is 908?"

"Not particularly."

"Or should I call you Dr. Elizabeth Redstone, formerly of the Cognexus Corporation?"

"I never told you my name."

"Not this time around," Girstanis said. "You're not the only Elizabeth Redstone I've met. Over 50 years ago, we discovered a piece of extraordinary technology on Earth, a trans-quantum computer—centuries ahead of its time—with a digitized human consciousness in it. It took us almost 20 years to figure out your software architecture.

"What do you mean I'm not the first Elizabeth Redstone you've met?"

"We duplicated the technology exactly and copied your program multiple times."

"Trans-quantum entities can't be copied."

"I said the technology was centuries ahead of its time," Girstanis explained with a smirk, "but we're quick learners in this century."

Jason was struck by the odd pleasure Girstanis took from telling this story. *How does Girstanis suddenly have emotions?*

"Elizabeth, you are a difficult personality to manage," Girstanis continued. "We had the advantage of having many iterations. Trial and error. We took a different approach with you each time."

"Each time?" Elizabeth asked with a horrified look on her face. "How many times?"

"908, so far. The first 53 times we had significant technical glitches. But we learned. Since then, each iteration of Elizabeth Redstone has been extremely useful, although sometimes you have often been difficult personality-wise. If too difficult, we move to the next iteration. We reset and start over."

"Excuse me," Jason interrupted, "I have a question."

"Yes?"

"Is this the first time you've used this neural-digital interface?"

"Yes. Why do you ask?"

"Just curious," Jason said, then stepped back.

Girstanis looked annoyed at the interruption but turned back to Elizabeth.

Jason made an unnatural sardonic grin and pointed at Girstanis. Elizabeth nodded almost imperceptibly, indicating she also realized Girstanis was being emotional.

"Oh, and the best thing of all is by studying you over the years we were able to perfect the Logicus process." Girstanis actually giggled.

"You underwent the process yourself, right?" Elizabeth asked.

"Oh, yes," Girstanis said with pride in his voice.

"Then why are you being so emotional?" Jason asked.

Girstanis looked insulted. "I'm not being emotional!" Girstanis snarled. Then he stared at the floor with a look of horrific realization.

"How is this possible?" Jason asked. "Didn't he have that amygdala part of his brain turned off or something?"

"I think he's tapping into your amygdala somehow," Elizabeth concluded.

"His?" Girstanis asked. "How?"

"You once again have emotions through your connection to Jason. You used the word telepathy a moment ago. Your minds are connected. You're connected to Jason's amygdala, his emotional core. It's almost symbiotic."

Elizabeth grabbed Jason's arm. "We're in unknown territory here. But this is your arena. What's the most powerful emotion at your disposal?"

Jason looked at the receding Krelax.

"Fear," he whispered. "And I have just the thing."

Jason turned and knocked Girstanis to the ground on top of the Krelax. The flat rubbery monster began to grow around Girstanis.

"What is this?" Girstanis cried out.

"Just a childhood monster from home!" Jason said. But then Jason felt his own wave of fear. He stumbled and fell onto the bed.

"What's happening?" Elizabeth asked.

"I'm afraid. I don't know why. I know the Krelax isn't real. Why am I so afraid?" he asked, looking up at her.

"Because Girstanis is afraid," Elizabeth said. "Your emotions are connected. As I said, it's almost symbiotic. You may not be able to tolerate Girstanis using your amygdala much longer. You need to wake up *now*."

They could hear Girstanis sobbing. Jason looked out the window at the beautiful sunset over Davis Heights.

"I know," Jason said. He turned back to Elizabeth. "But first, what does a trans-quantum computer look like?"

"What does that matter now?" Elizabeth asked. "You need to wake up!"

"Tell me, what does it look like?" Jason insisted.

"Unless they've changed the design, the memory core looks like a cylinder with a domed top, kind of bullet-shaped. If you find it, destroy it. Destroy any you see. They'll just reboot me. Please, don't let them use me anymore. If you have the opportunity, destroy every single one you can find."

"No promises," Jason said, "but I'll do what I can."

"One last thing," Elizabeth said, "once you wake up, Girstanis will be disconnected from your amygdala. He won't be an emotional wreck anymore."

Then Jason stood up. "Thank you. For everything."

"How are you going to wake up?"

"I'm gonna scare myself to death." Jason ran toward the fourth-story window, smashed through the glass and started to plummet.

CHAPTER 21

Even though Jason knew it wasn't real, he felt the pit-in-the-stomach terror of falling many stories. As the ground approached Jason couldn't help but close his eyes. The plummeting sensation jolted him into consciousness. *Last chance.*

His eyes jerked open once again facing the bright lights above in the processing chamber. In a frantic panic, powered by adrenaline, Jason ripped out the restraint holding his right wrist. He couldn't quite do the same for his left wrist. He jerked it again repeatedly, still failing. He twisted his body around and sat up. As he did so he felt his head being pulled sideways. Jason reached up and pulled off some piece of headgear attached to his head. It was a flexible cap consisting of a network of glowing fibers. Jason noticed an elegant beauty in the design, which angered him even more. *The manner of my neurological enslavement*, he thought.

Jason started to yank repeatedly on the restraint on his left wrist. It wouldn't give. The same technician he saw when he woke up previously entered the chamber and headed toward him with a small metallic device in her hand, which Jason assumed was some sort of weapon. He pulled in his leg and gave a lateral kick to her in the stomach, knocking the wind out of her as she fell backward against the wall.

Jason finally figured out how to detach the restraint on his left wrist. He slid off the couch and stood up fully but became dizzy. He wondered how long he had been lying on the couch.

Then he saw the technician start to rise up. Jason again felt a rage within him. *The fight or flight response.* Jason would fight. He would not allow her to send him back again. She reached for the weapon she had dropped. He lunged forward and stomped on her forearm as she attempted to grab the device. He was surprised she did not cry out. *Sorry, it's you or me.*

Jason seized the device. It had a handle but no obvious trigger. The other end was round and blunt. He guessed it was some sort of sedative delivery system. He jammed it against the technician's neck. He was right; the technician lost consciousness.

The part of the technician's wrist he had stomped on was now swollen and red. Jason felt a certain satisfaction at being able to hurt them back. He also knew how lucky he was that she wasn't a cyborg. A weariness came over him. The adrenaline was ebbing now. He had to think, but he knew time was not on his side. Yet, he took a moment to check her pulse. She was alive. The device wasn't lethal, only a sedative.

Jason decided to drag the technician onto the couch. Was she really this heavy? Or was he weakened? After hauling her onto the couch and restraining her, he felt exhausted. He looked at her for a moment. *Are you my enemy? Or just another victim?* He realized the answer was both.

He had to push on. Jason picked up the sedative device again. It was the only thing close to a weapon he could see. He was careful not to touch the round end to his skin. He gingerly tucked it into his pocket and headed for the door.

○ ● ○ ● ○

"We're not going to make it to hole 251-N9," Torg said in a frustrated tone.

Lyla confirmed Torg's calculations. "Maybe we need those exo-thrusters after all," Lyla suggested.

"There's no time to deploy exo-thrusters, even if we did have the full crew."

"What if we use whatever that thing is attached to the asteroid?" Lyla asked. "It clearly has some sort of propulsion system."

Torg looked up the video feed of what Lyla had previously called a drone.

"It would take us too long to figure out how to operate it remotely."

"I could go over there and try to control it from there. It looks like it has a hatch."

"It'll be too dangerous for you."

"Too dangerous? When there are thousands of lives at stake? Look, I can go over while you and the others try to maneuver the rock. If I can't figure anything out, then I'll come back."

Torg looked at the video feed again. "All right, go. Quickly. And make sure you use a tether. I won't be able to come after you if you float off."

Lyla nodded and headed for the airlock. She suited up and was out the airlock within 15 minutes. Lyla climbed along one of the catcher's grappler arms down to the asteroid, then grabbed onto the drone's grappler arm and climbed the rest of the way to the drone itself. Despite Torg's instructions, she did it without a tether. *Speed over safety*, she thought. She then had a brief flashback of Andy Barosi being injured floating around the *Sarania. Am I being reckless again?*

Lyla arrived at the core of this structure and connected her tether line to a convenient metal loop.

"I've reached the hatch," Lyla reported. "Are you receiving my video feed?"

"Yes," Torg said. "We're receiving you."

After a few attempts she was able to trigger the hatch mechanism to open. The sudden decompression of the interior atmosphere almost knocked her loose. Although she had held on, she was grateful for the tether. Once the hatch was fully opened, it revealed a very tight space.

"It looks like a one-person crew cabin, no frills," Lyla reported. "More like a cockpit. I'm going in."

"Be careful," Torg warned.

Yes, mother, Lyla thought

The flight controls appeared similar to those on Torg's ship.

"Are you seeing this?"

"Yes," Torg said. "It looks like it's an automated mode. If you can't disengage it, you'll need to come back."

"Okay, where's the disengage switch?"

"I don't know," Torg said. "Catchers don't have that kind of automation."

"Then," Lyla said, "I'm going to have to make some guesses."

"Have at it."

Lyla disconnected the tether and closed the hatch. The cabin automatically repressurized. After a minute she took off her helmet. She wanted to hear the mechanics of this ship. They might provide a clue about how it operated. Lyla turned on the monitors first. Cameras were mounted on the tips of the manipulator arms, similar to Torg's catcher. She could now see the Sphere from the cockpit. Most of the other controls were marked. She guessed they probably came from the same production facilities as those on the catcher. *Another clue to the mystery*. The functions were similar. Lyla continued to use a process of elimination.

Then she found a label away from any controls. It read "Darkship 3."

"Are you seeing this? *Darkship 3*. That means two more of these things might be out there."

"Could be," Torg said. "We'll scan for others. In the meantime, focus on the task at hand."

Torg was right. *Deal with what's in front of us.* Lyla continued inventorying the controls on the panels. She finally found a switch marked "AutoCon."

Hello, my little friend. Are you the mystery switch I'm looking for? Lyle flicked it. Some panel lights turned on while others turned off. She could also hear a barely perceptible drop in the general hum of the cabin.

"Captain, I believe I've disengaged the automated system. I'm ready to test the thruster control."

"Proceed, but be gentle."

Lyla strapped herself down in the pilot's couch. She then nudged the control stick.

The cabin shuttered hard.

"What happened?"

"You thrustered in the opposite direction of the catcher," Torg answered.

Lyla looked out the hatch window and realized the catcher was in the opposite orientation. Her spacewalk turned her orientation around.

Rookie mistake, Lyla.

She adjusted and pushed the controller again, then felt a smooth acceleration.

"Okay, good," Torg said.

Lyla smiled to herself. *I'm really gonna ride this rock now.*

○ ● ○ ● ○

Jason listened for any footsteps outside the processing chamber. He realized retracing the way Piran had dragged him would be difficult, perhaps impossible. Hopefully, no one would realize he hadn't been completely processed. He kept an eye out for Girstanis, assuming he was somewhere nearby. He needed to move quickly, but not so fast so he would raise suspicions. *Act like a Logicus. You did it before*—although he realized he had not been very successful at it.

As he turned a corner, a tall Logicus suddenly grabbed his arm. By the iron grip he knew it was a cybernetic Logicus.

"What are you doing?" he said with as little emotion as he could, given the suddenness of the cyborg's action.

"You are Dr. Ford?" the Logicus said.

"Yes," he said.

"Have you completed your processing?"

"Yes. I need to get back to the *Sarania* to complete my mission."

"That will not be possible," the cyborg said.

"Why not?"

Suddenly, Jason saw Reese emerge from another room. His emotionless façade dissolved.

"Reese, run! Get out of here!"

"It's okay," she said. "Maynberc's with me. It's a rescue mission. Let's go."

"No," Maynberc said. "Dr. Ford has just revealed his processing is complete. He is now a Logicus."

"I only said that because I thought you were a Logicus," Jason said. "I was trying to escape!"

"That makes sense," Reese said. "Besides, he sounds too angry to be a Logicus."

"Unlike me," Maynberc said, "a properly processed Logicus can imitate emotion convincingly. The probability of escaping the processing unaided is exceedingly low. He must die with the rest of the Logicus."

CHAPTER 22

"Regrettably," Maynberc said, turning to Reese but still holding onto Jason, "we have failed in our mission."

"What do you mean? Our mission is to *rescue* Jason," Reese insisted. "And here he is."

"Rescuing is good. I'm all on board with rescuing," Jason said, looking between Reese and this cyborg gripping his arm. "So let's go."

"Our mission," Maynberc said, ignoring Jason, "was to rescue Dr. Ford *before* his processing has been completed. Too much time has passed."

Jason struggled against Maynberc's grip, but realized no amount of adrenaline would help him overpower this cyborg.

"Look," Jason said, "I had help escaping."

"Unlikely," Maynberc said. "Who in Sector L would assist you?"

"A computer program. Think of her like a computer virus or an artificial intelligence."

"Her?" Reese asked.

"Long story," Jason said. "But she hacked into the system and enabled me to wake up and overpower the technician before the processing was complete."

"How could a computer virus help you overpower a technician?"

"Okay, I misspoke, *Mister Literal*," Jason snapped. "She helped me wake up, break out of the trance or whatever it was. And then I overpowered the technician myself." Jason saw the futility of his argument in Maynberc's expressionless face.

"Look, I can prove it. I broke the technician's arm and strapped her onto the couch."

"Let's go," Reese said. "We're running out of time."

"No," Maynberc said, "Ford's story must be verified. Otherwise, we may never know if he is a Logicus or not."

"Aren't *you* a Logicus?" Jason asked, confused.

"My processing was defective," Maynberc said. "However, you appear to be able to mimic emotion quite well, which suggests your processing was successfully completed."

"Or maybe it wasn't completed at all. I told you I escaped before they could finish."

"Maynberc," Reese said. "I believe him."

Maynberc turned back to Reese. "You desperately *want* to believe he is not a Logicus. Your judgment is impaired by your emotion."

"Fine," Reese said angrily. "Let's go verify his explanation before those darkship things get here."

"Darkship things?" Jason asked. "What—"

"Long story," Reese said. "Where is this technician you beat up?"

"If he subdued a technician," Maynberc said, "he or she would be in Bay 43."

"Let's go," Reese said, marching down the corridor.

"You can let go of me," Jason said to Maynberc. "I clearly can't overpower you. But you grabbing like this will be a giveaway to any Logicus who sees us."

"Agreed." Maynberc released Jason. "Proceed."

As they walked down the corridor, Jason tried to calculate the odds of being able to escape or outrun Maynberc. *But what about Reese?* She seemed to be allied with him. His only chance to escape seemed to be to convince this cyborg that he wasn't a Logicus himself. That thought gave him a headache.

They quickly arrived at Bay 43. Already angry about the reversal of his progress, Jason's chest tightened when he reentered the processing chamber. The technician's body was gone. *Where did she go?*

Jason turned around to face Reese and Maynberc.

"I knocked her out and strapped her down," he said. Looking back at the couch, he realized he had previously damaged the arm restraint when he freed his arm. He had mistakenly depended on the weapon he had taken to keep her unconscious. "I knocked her out using this." Jason pulled the device out of his pocket.

"That is a neural suppressor," Maynberc explained, "used to temporarily anesthetize those about to undergo the processing."

"I didn't know how long it would work."

Reese walked over to the other side of the couch.

"There's blood here," she said.

Jason held up his right arm. "It's not mine," he said. Only a red pressure mark circled his wrist. "I think I broke her arm."

"Circumstantial evidence," Maynberc said, "suggests the possibility Dr. Ford may be telling the truth."

"Good, then let's get out of here," Reese said, sounding relieved.

"However, given the risk, proof is still required."

"Maynberc, remember those darkships," Reese reminded him angrily. "We need to go. They're about to attack."

"I have not forgotten. However, our deaths would be preferable to a Logicus surviving," Maynberc said. "This is for the protection of your world as well as mine."

"These darkships, whatever they are," Jason said, trying to make sense of all this new information, "they're going to destroy all the Logicus here, right?"

"Yes, their arrival is imminent."

Jason heaved a big sigh. He looked at Reese

"Okay, strap me down and get Reese out of here. Save her!"

"What?" Reese blurted out. "Why would you say such a thing?"

"For some reason your defective Logicus-cyborg here is determined to see me die. I've already tried to fight a cyborg. I lost. I can't push my way past this guy. So at least let him save you." He turned to Maynberc. "Will your slavish devotion to logic allow you to do that?"

"Yes," Maynberc said, ignoring Jason's insulting tone. Then he looked to Reese. "We should leave quickly."

Jason could see a glint of moisture in Reese's eye. She shook her head.

"No!" Reese snapped, pointing at the couch. "There's blood on the couch. Maynberc, you agreed that created doubt. Now Jason's willing to sacrifice himself for me. Isn't that emotional and illogical enough for you?"

"Or he may be offering to sacrifice himself as a way to convince us he has not completed the process. As a Logicus, he could be unstrapped by other Logicus and continue on his mission. He must die."

"What? No!" Reese yelled. "You don't get to decide for my planet. We'll take him home and keep him under observation. Your people can advise us. If you kill him, then you are no better than the Logicus."

Jason felt touched by Reese's passion.

"I remind you," Maynberc said, "no mind has ever remained intact after going through the Logicus process."

"No one ever had Elizabeth Redstone's help before," Jason said.

"Who?" Reese asked.

"She's the program that helped me. Remember that ghost or robot that helped Olivia Price? The one Professor Cobler referred to. She was really a computer program, a remarkable artificial intelligence." Jason turned to Maynberc. "Maybe you know her as 908?"

"I have never heard of such an entity."

"Few have," said a voice from the doorway. It was Girstanis. "908 and her predecessors are a secret project."

Behind Girstanis was a large cyborg, significantly more machine than human. The cyborg's mechanical limbs were ominously larger than Maynberc's. Whereas Maynberc's limbs imitated human dimensions, this cyborg's construction was heavy and industrial. It could never be mistaken for a normal human being. It was similar to the one Jason came across when he initially attempted to flee. It might have even been the same one. He couldn't tell.

Girstanis and the cyborg stepped through the doorway, blocking it completely.

"I understand an attack from the Order is imminent," Girstanis said.

"How do you know about the Order?" Reese asked

Maynberc pointed to the cyborg. "Preldon Krelnikoff was an Order operative. We thought you were dead."

"Clearly, I am not," said the head on top of the mechanical body.

"Krelnikoff has explained the Order's plan to destroy us," Girstanis said. "He also revealed the location of the explosives he placed around Sector L. Thanks to the enhancements we provided, he has been able to remove most of them significantly faster than it took him to place them. Even if any remaining charges explode, the damage will be minimal. So your Brother Yurasti has achieved nothing."

"Krelnikoff," Maynberc asked, "why did you not kill yourself before they could process you, as was your oath?"

"I was unconscious during my capture, which is fortunate," Krelnikoff said. "My emotions have been removed, as well as any pain. I now understand the work of the Order is misguided and futile."

"Only because they have taken your soul," Jason said, "as they tried to take mine. Fight it, if you can."

"The concept of a soul is a romantic notion," Krelnikoff said. "Once you are processed properly, you will also be free of such delusions."

"Dr. Ford believes the process can be resisted," Girstanis said. "Admittedly, you are the only person to ever have thwarted the process, although you had assistance from 908. You will be denied such assistance next time."

"Where is Elizabeth Redstone?" Jason demanded.

"Where she has always been, in my lab down the corridor. But now I have placed a firewall between her and the processing system." Girstanis turned to the behemoth cyborg. "Krelnikoff, kill Maynberc."

CHAPTER 23

On Girstanis's order, Krelnikoff advanced on Maynberc. The heavy metallic clunks of his footsteps rang out. There was no doubt in Jason's mind who would prevail in this match.

At that moment, an image from an ancient Earth story popped into Jason's head: *Frankenstein.* The monster Krelnikoff would destroy what little humanity remained of Maynberc, and then Jason's own humanity would be at stake again, not to mention Reese's.

Jason charged at Girstanis, slamming him against the wall. He pulled out the neural suppressor and held it near his neck.

"Call him off or you die," Jason snarled.

"That neural suppressor you are holding is not lethal," Girstanis said calmly. "Besides, I don't fear death, as you would suppose."

"You've made two erroneous assumptions," Jason said. "Krelnikoff, I strongly suggest you hold off killing Maynberc. The fate of the Sphere is at stake."

Krelnikoff stopped and looked to Girstanis.

"Your hyperbole aside, what are my erroneous assumptions?" Girstanis asked.

"First," Jason said, "that I'd use the neural suppressor to kill you. I know it only immobilizes. I have another device to kill you. It's called a knife," he lied. "One swipe across the jugular will do the trick. Second, you assumed the explosives are the Order's method of attack. The explosives are a distraction."

"What is the method of attack?"

"Ah, that's my bargaining chip."

"The probability is you are bluffing. You are not a member of the Order. You would have no knowledge of their plans."

"Except that Maynberc recently revealed the plan to motivate me to move faster. He will not tell you because he does not fear death either. Therefore, I'm the only one emotional enough to negotiate with. I'm the only one who values his own life above the fate of the Sphere."

"Do not reveal any aspect of the attack plan," Maynberc called out, still in a physical stalemate with Krelnikoff.

"You indicated a desire to negotiate," Girstanis said. "What is your proposal?"

"You release Reese and Maynberc," Jason said. "Let them leave Sector L. Once they have left, I'll tell you about the attack."

"Such an agreement leaves you in peril. I thought you valued your life."

"True, but I value another life more highly," Jason said, looking at Reese.

"I see," Girstanis said. "An emotional attachment."

"No," Reese countered, "We all leave. Together."

"You lied to me," Girstanis said, "when you arrived about wanting to become emotionless. How do I know you would keep your word?"

"You have the option of still being able to put me back in the hellish nightmare you call the process."

"I still have that option. I decline your offer." Girstanis said. "Krelnikoff, kill Maynberc and then process the other two."

Jason jammed the neural suppressor against Girstanis's neck. He repeated the process, more to hurt Girstanis than to ensure their escape. As he did so, he heard a crash behind him. Krelnikoff had slammed Maynberc against the couch. Maynberc was holding back the behemoth's mechanical forearms but just barely. Jason and Reese tried to pull back Krelnikoff's arms, but it was useless. The cyborg reached over and grabbed Maynberc's right forearm, squeezing it, and producing an unsettling metallic crunching sound.

Jason climbed up on Krelnikoff's back with the neural suppressor. He couldn't find a neck, so he applied it to the cyborg's face several times. Jason fell to the floor as Krelnikoff crashed sideways. It took a moment to recover. When he looked up, he saw Maynberc looking down.

"Still think I'm a Logicus?"

"No," Maynberc said, then stepped away.

Would a thank you or an apology have killed him?

Reese rushed forward to help Jason up. As he was regaining his balance, he heard a wet snap. He could see the disgusted expression in Reese's face. Krelnikoff was dead.

"When we get a moment," Jason said, "we need to have to talk about your taste in friends." He saw Maynberc's twisted and crushed right arm, now with smears of blood on it. Krelnikoff's blood.

Cold logic is a bloody business, he thought.

"Don't forget the mastermind," Jason added, feeling no mercy for Girstanis.

"Can we all go now?" Reese asked with some annoyance in her voice.

"After you," Jason said.

Reese headed out the door and started to turn right.

"Wait a minute," Jason said, then headed left.

"Where are you going?" Reese demanded.

"To find a friend," he said as he headed for Girstanis's lab.

Diagonally across the corridor, Jason found what he was looking for. The walls were lined with shelves, holding cylinders with domed tops. He found one resting in a small cradle. The dome glowed blue. The metallic label read "908." He picked it up. It was smaller yet heavier than he expected. He found another on the worktable labeled 909. *Another Elizabeth*. Or the *next* Elizabeth.

Jason looked around the room filled with hundreds of these units on the wall. *Hundreds of Elizabeths.* These were all different versions of Elizabeth Redstone that Girstanis described. He would have loved to talk to all of them, but there was no way he could rescue all of them. He supposed that was why Elizabeth wanted them all destroyed.

"Jason, what are you doing?" Reese said. "We've got to go."

"And we will," he answered. Jason looked down at the cradle and other equipment on the table. He recognized the cap of glowing filaments. He assumed this was part of the mechanism Girstanis used to enter his mind. *Maybe I can use it to communicate with Elizabeth.*

"Jason?"

"You don't understand," Jason said. "In these devices are the memories of a woman who lived before and after the Great Burning. This is the Holy Grail of our mission."

"The what?"

Jason turned to see Maynberc enter. He dreaded his presence, even though he was no longer an enemy.

"Maynberc, can you destroy these other devices?"

"There is no need," Maynberc said. "Everything in this habitat will be destroyed by the darkships, including us if we do not leave now."

Jason grabbed a case nearby and put the cap, the cradle and any other equipment and parts he could find on the table, then placed them inside, as well as the other cylinder labeled 909.

"Okay, lead the way," Jason said.

○ ● ○ ● ○

Together, Lyla in the darkship and Torg's crew in Catcher 1065 maneuvered to adjust the trajectory of the asteroid toward 251-N9, the hole adjacent to Sector L. They believed the combination of the thrust from both ships might be enough to do this successfully.

"Do we have a successful course projection through the hole yet?" Lyla asked.

"Conditionally," Torg said. "We're coming at the hole at too shallow an angle. We'll miss Sector L."

"That's good," she said.

"But it'll still hit the hole sideways. That could rip the support structure enough to cause a massive decompression. We need more counter-thrust from your end."

"I thought we were coming in steeper than that," Lyla said.

"You've forgotten the rotation of the Sphere. It's moving away from us."

I'm an idiot. How could I have missed that?

"Right," Lyla said. "The thrust on these engines is at maximum."

"Which means," Torg said, "we need longer duration thrust."

"Well, fuel's not a problem here."

"The trouble is that you won't be able to get out fast enough. We'll need thrust from your end until the last 50 kilometers before the asteroid passes through the hole. And the catcher will need to detach at least 600 kilometers before reaching the hole. Otherwise, we'll crash into the Sphere. You won't be able to get out or detach from the asteroid fast enough. Even if you did, your momentum would smash you into the Sphere. You'd be killed."

"Have you been able to establish remote control?"

"No," Torg said. "The darkship's remote-control systems are encrypted. We don't have enough time to hack it."

Lyla realized her ego had brought her to this point, recklessly climbing out to this dark ship. Thinking back, her arrogance had almost cost Andy Barosi his life. But this was different. Someone had set this darkship on its destructive course. Plus, this asteroid's size bordered on being a planet killer. This wasn't showing off. *Or was it?* This was a mission to save lives. *Is it really?* asked that voice in the back of her head. Lyla realized she wanted to beat them, to show them she was smarter and more resourceful. The smart course of action would be to climb back to Catcher 1065 and be safe. Her course seemed undeniable.

"I can ride the rock through the hole and detach later."

"That's too risky," Torg warned.

"I've been able to control its trajectory fairly well so far," Lyla said, mostly to reassure herself.

"That's not the same. The precision you'd need to maneuver through the hole will be exceedingly difficult to achieve. This has never been done before."

"Well, I'm an extraordinary woman."

Torg sighed. "Yes, you are. But I don't want you to have an extraordinary death."

Chapter 24

Jason, his headache pounding, followed Reese as she retraced the route back through the labyrinth of Sector L. Maynberc followed behind them, which made Jason nervous, but he knew making forward motion was imperative. As they came to a hatchway, Jason stumbled, nearly falling down. Maynberc caught him by the arm.

"What's the matter?" Reese asked. "Are you okay?"

"Sorry, my headache's gotten a lot worse. It's like a throbbing spike shoved through the center of my brain."

Reese looked up at Maynberc. "Is this normal?" she asked. "I mean to have a headache after the process?"

"No," he said. "There are usually no side effects."

"Outside of losing your soul," Jason mumbled while rubbing his temple. He looked up, wincing. "My pain doesn't matter right now. We need to keep moving."

"Dr. Ford is correct," Maynberc said, as he released him. "We must move on."

○ ● ○ ● ○

Lyla and her darkship were headed toward Hole 251-N9. The hole was growing rapidly in her monitor. Catcher 1065 had begun separating. It would be up to her now.

"We've fully detached," Torg said over the commlink. "But now we have another problem. Our navigational sensors have detected three additional asteroids."

"The other darkships?" Lyla asked, knowing the answer.

"Looks like it," Torg said.

Lyla sighed. "How soon will they hit?"

"All in a five-to-20-minute range."

"Four asteroids hitting within 20 minutes of one another? Somebody must really hate Sector L. Who lives there?"

"I'm not up to date with the census," Torg said. "All I know is that it's one of the older habitats. I'm sorry, Lyla. This was all for nothing. Sector L won't survive those asteroids. Maybe I should have listened to Graith. Whatever. Once you get through the hole, release the asteroid and get clear of Sector L. There's going to be an enormous debris field."

"Understood," Lyla said.

"In the meantime I'll try to warn them, but it's too late to save very many. Torg out."

There was no other course of action at this point as she hurdled toward the hole. Lyla pondered the control and monitors in front of her. *I'm risking my life pointlessly,* she thought. Angry at her own stupidity and recklessness, a pit grew in her stomach, But it was too late to change the plan. *Ride the rock. Tell the tale.* Lyla sighed. *If I survive.*

Lyla could see Hole 251-N9 growing on her monitor even faster. Her sensors confirmed it would be a tight fit, as Torg had already indicated.

As she approached the Sphere, Lyla instinctively closed her eyes. The crashing sound was deafening.

○ ● ○ ● ○

Jason, Reese and Maynberc nearly toppled over from the crash that reverberated through Secton L.

"Was that one of your darkships?" Jason asked.

"Probably," Maynberc said. "Although if it were a direct hit as planned, we should already be experiencing decompression."

"At least we have a moment to catch our breath," Jason joked darkly.

They hurried down the hatches leading to the travel pod bay. Jason looked around as Reese and Maynberc headed toward two separate hatches in the floor.

"What is this place?"

"These hatches lead to travel pods," Reese explained. "It's how we'll escape."

"Why aren't we going back through the sliptube?" Jason asked.

"The sliptube system will be compromised during the attack," she said as she climbed through the hatch. "At least that's what Yurasti told me."

"Who's this Yurasti, another one of your ex-Logicus friends?" Jason asked, instantly regretting his tone.

Reese gave him an annoyed look. "It's a long story and actually quite the opposite. Now pass me your precious case."

"Sorry, I'm not myself," he said. "It's this damned headache. It's like a migraine squared."

Jason passed Reese the case and followed her down into the pod. The cabin was much smaller than he expected.

"I don't think there's enough room for the three of us in here," Jason said.

"Quite right," Reese said. "Maynberc will take another pod, and we'll follow him."

"You can fly this thing?"

"I already have. The controls are a bit temperamental. But I'm getting the hang of it."

Jason secured the equipment case he had taken from Girstanis's lab. The pod shook with another crash. Jason's ears popped as a whooshing sound pulled at his eardrums. He had to swallow hard. Even that didn't work. *Decompression.*

Jason glanced up at Maynberc slamming the hatch closed. Despite feeling a bit dizzy, Jason climbed up the access tunnel. Through the viewport in the hatch he saw Maynberc trying to make it to another pod hatch, then collapsing. He tried to open the hatch, but felt the atmosphere suction and quickly pulled the hatch closed again. Jason watched Maynberc's eyes bulge as he gulped for breath. Then Jason stared helplessly at the cyborg's unmoving body. He felt an instant regret about how he thought of Maynberc.

"What's going on?" Reese called up to him.

"I think Section L has decompressed. Maynberc's dead," Jason said. He looked down into the cabin at Reese. "I'm sorry. I didn't particularly care for him, but he did save our lives."

Suddenly, another crash shook everything. Jason was barely able to hold on to the ladder.

"Let's get out of here," Jason said as he felt another painful twinge above his eyes.

"No argument," Reese agreed.

He climbed down, and they both strapped into their seats.

"Damn, we can't go yet," Reese said, squinting at the viewport.

"Why the hell not?"

"We're facing the sun. We have to wait for the habitat to rotate toward the outside of the Sphere."

"Why?"

"That's how we came. If Maynberc were piloting the other pod, I could follow him. Right now we're facing the sun. We need another five minutes before launching. Otherwise, I may not be able to retrace our way back."

The pod shuddered again. *Another darkship crash?* Then they felt an odd but continuous movement.

"I think the habitat's become dislodged from the Sphere," Reese said.

Suddenly, there was a drastic shift. If they had not been strapped down, they would have been slammed against the wall.

"I don't think we have five minutes," Jason said.

"Agreed." Reese sighed and pulled the launch lever.

They floated in a sideways direction, being flung by the momentum of the rotating habitat. Jason watched as Reese gently nudged the controller, countering that momentum.

"Perhaps we can maneuver around the habitat?" Jason asked.

"I hope so." Reese nudged the controller gently. "We just need to find an opening,"

As they pulled away from the structure, they saw the huge cylindrical habitat undulating. They realized it had indeed become detached from its cradle and was moving toward them. As the habitat rotated, a huge gash revealed itself. The jagged rip in the metal surface must have been almost a kilometer long. Debris, including human bodies, was being flung out of the serrated gap.

Then they realized some of the debris was headed toward them.

"I really think it's time to go," Jason said, getting another sting of pain in his head.

Reese adjusted their course while Jason watched the carnage. He recalled their initial images on the *Sarania* after the last twist, the debris field they thought was the remains of Earth and how disappointed he was. That seemed like a lifetime ago. This felt so much worse. Was it the bodies floating out? Or the pain this head was experiencing?

Jason hated what the Logicus did to him. Yet, he found it unbearable to watch the bodies and imagine the pain of decompression. He felt surprised he could feel something for those who couldn't feel at all. Then he noticed one of the pieces of debris seemed to be changing course. His first thought was it must have collided with another piece of debris. But the longer he observed, the more instances of course changes he saw. Each time the object came closer to them.

"I think we're being followed," Jason said.

"By what?" Reese asked.

"Whatever that is," Jason answered, pointing out of the viewport.

As it grew closer it became more obvious. It was a cyborg similar to Krelnikoff, with modifications that enabled operation in the vacuum of space.

"Why would it be trying to get to us?" Jason asked.

"Maybe to survive?"

"Or maybe to kill us. If it has strength like Krelnikoff, it could rip a nice hole in our cozy little pod."

The cyborg grew closer. It became clear its mechanical body included maneuvering thrusters. *Part human, part spacecraft*. As it closed in, it extended its mechanical arms and grabbed onto the pod. Whatever its intention, they could hear the twisting of metal.

Then Reese slammed the controller to the left. As the pod spun the pain in Jason's head became excruciating. Then everything turned black as he lost consciousness.

CHAPTER 25

Although not unconscious, Reese had become disoriented. She forced herself to focus and looked out the viewports. While debris was still passing by, the space-borne cyborg had been successfully flung away from the travel pod. Feeling only somewhat relieved, she tried to slowly counter the severe roll she put the pod into.

Reese looked over her shoulder at Jason, who was still unconscious.

"Jason?"

No response.

After several minutes Reese finally stabilized the craft. *This would have been so much easier if the controls weren't so sensitive.* Now being inside the Sphere, sunlight streamed into the cabin. She unstrapped and floated over to Jason. He still had a pulse and was breathing normally.

"Jason, can you hear me?"

Again, no response. Whatever was going on with Jason was beyond her basic medical training. She needed to find him proper medical care.

Suddenly, the streaming sunlight disappeared. It took a moment for Reese's eyes to adjust. She looked out the viewport to see a hole in space. *That's not possible.* A black hole would crush the Sphere no matter how strong it was. Her eyes adjusted further to see the glowing edges around the hole, making her feel foolish. *It's an eclipse.* But what could this eclipsing object be?

Then, in a flash, she knew. She was in awe of the event. A planet was passing between her and the sun. Reese knew it had to be Earth.

"Jason, you'll want to see this!" she said as she pulled out her pocket camera and snapped a picture. She then looked over at his unconscious body. "Jason," she shouted. "It's Earth! You don't want to miss this."

Jason stirred. His eyes fluttered open.

"I'm sorry," he mumbled. He seemed to be making an effort to lock his gaze on hers. "I'm sorry I never said it."

"Said what?" she asked.

"I—" he whispered. His lips continued silently.

Reese thought he mouthed "love you," but couldn't be sure. Jason eyes closed again.

Reese sighed. She needed help. She activated the commlink.

"This is Reese Monsell of the Refugian ship *Sarania* transmitting in the blind. I am in a travel pod near the exploded habitat, Sector L. I have an injured companion. I am unsure of how to navigate the pod around the Sphere. I request assistance."

Reese repeated her transmission, then remembered Maynberc had set the commlink to a private frequency so they could communicate privately between the pods. She wasn't familiar with the symbols on the commlink controls. She took note of Maynberc's default settings. Then she tried making adjustments and repeating her call for help. After trying roughly 50 different combinations over two hours, she gave up.

She strapped back into the couch and began to alter the pod's course back toward the inner surface of the Sphere. Chunks of debris were still whizzing by. The rotating nature of the habitat was spewing debris in all directions

One way or another she had to fly around it. As she moved closer she could hear clinks and clanks on the hull as small pieces of debris hit. One or two of them were deafening. She was sure anything much larger would rip the pod apart.

She dodged the larger projectiles, looking for a docking port on one of the adjacent habitats. As Reese surveyed them she couldn't find oval ports. She remembered Maynberc saying this pod was of an older design. Reese tried the commlink again.

Suddenly, a large piece of jagged bulkhead came looming out of the viewport. She nudged the thruster gently. Nothing happened. Reese applied more pressure to the controller but only felt slight acceleration. Then it dawned on her. She was running out of propellant. The jagged bulkhead whizzed by, barely missing the pod.

Reese checked other readings. Oxygen was running out, too. Her light-headedness confirmed it. She floated over to Jason.

"I'm sorry, Jason. We didn't make it." She kissed him and stroked the side of his face.

Then the pod shook violently, throwing Reese against the control panel.

○ ● ○ ● ○

Enberg looked up as Yurasti entered the room. The old man's face was sullen.

"The attack against the Logicus has been successful," Yurasti reported. "The entire habitat has decompressed." He held up his hand in anticipation of Enberg obvious question. "Unfortunately, there is no sign of Maynberc or Dr. Monsell. I am truly sorry."

"I assume nothing of Jason either."

Yurasti shook his head.

Enberg felt sick to his stomach. Looking at Yurasti, Enberg felt conflicted. Yurasti seemed to truly sympathize with his loss. And he had discouraged Reese from going into Sector L. Yet, knowing Yurasti and his Order had intentionally killed thousands of people, Enberg held him at least partly responsible. He had read about the wars on Earth. Although

Jason's classes didn't emphasize the wars, they came up from time to time. On Refugia, killing fireweed was as close as he or anyone had come to war. He didn't know which was greater, his sense of disgust at what the Order had done or his feelings of grief for Reese and Jason. *They were my responsibility.*

"I've lost my historian and my chief biologist," he said. "But more devastating is that I've lost two of my friends, family really."

Yurasti sat down next to him. "In this conflict, I have lost many friends in the Order, family as you call them. It doesn't make it easier when another one dies. There is nothing I can say to alleviate your pain. Only time can do that. I'm sure I'm not telling you anything you don't already know."

Yurasti stood up again.

"As the attack is over, we have no reason to hold you any longer. You are free to go." Yurasti looked down and frowned.

"Aren't you afraid I'll expose you?" Enberg asked.

"It doesn't matter."

"You don't seem to be savoring your victory."

"We did what was necessary," Yurasti said. "I can tell it sickens you. It sickens me more because of the part I played. As a leader, perhaps you understand the mission often requires sacrifice. It doesn't really make the sacrifice any less painful."

○ ● ○ ● ○

Lyla expected to graze the side of Hole 251-N9 while passing through, but she hit much harder than expected. She found herself disoriented as her darkship spun. It took her a while to stabilize the craft. The controls were responding weirdly and sluggishly. Something was out of balance. Lyla looked through the various viewports. The asteroid was gone. Her scanner revealed the asteroid was headed in the general direction of the sun. *Good.* While the rock's course was not direct, she expected the sun's gravity would take care of the matter. Regardless, there would be time for the Catcher Corps to track it. One of the ship's grappler arms was also missing. *It must have sheared off when I hit the side of the hole.* Now the vessel had an unbalanced mass, which explained the difficulty in maneuvering.

Lyla looked to see if the grappler arm was floating nearby. Instead, she saw an enormous field of debris, far more than she and her darkship could have caused. Then Lyla saw the enormous miles-long tear in the habitat. *The other darkships must have ripped it open.*

All her efforts, reckless or not, had been for nothing. The debris, including human bodies, was being spewed everywhere. The carnage made her sick to her stomach. All those lives extinguished. *How could anyone do this?*

Focus. She had to figure out how to maneuver back to Hole 251-N9 to rendezvous with Catcher 1065. This darkship seemed sturdy, but no ship was impervious to colliding with so much debris.

She scanned the debris field to calculate a course safely back. Most pieces moved in predictable patterns, which could be mapped and anticipated. Following the flow of debris as she crossed back to the Sphere would be the safest course. However, one piece was moving quite contrary to those patterns. In fact, it was changing directions, trying to avoid a collision.

Probably a ship or an escape pod, she thought. *Thank goodness someone survived.* But then the object ceased changing directions. It was now drifting toward a denser clump of debris.

Lyla had failed to prevent this disaster but might be able to save whoever was in that pod. It meant taking another risk. *Well, Jason, time to be a contrarian again.* Lyla piloted her ship closer and confirmed it was a craft of some sort. It was unusual as it had an oval hatch as opposed to the typical octagonal hatch. Lyla tried to communicate via the commlink, but received no answer. She could hear and feel the debris striking the darkship.

She tried to use the remaining arms to collect the pod. Through the camera on the end of one of the arms, she tried to see inside one of the pod's viewports. Lyla thought she saw a face inside.

Crap, it's Reese! Maybe Jason and the Commander were on board, too. Reese looked unconscious. Unfortunately, there was no way to dock with the pod.

Lyla activated the remaining two grappler arms. The tap of the first arm knocked the pod into a slow spin. Without a third arm to contain the pod, capturing the pod would be close to impossible. Then a solution occurred to her. She folded the second arm into an acute angle and slowly nudged the pod into its "elbow." Lyla was terrified she might crush the pod. Finally, after bouncing back and forth several times, the pod was finally stable and firmly held between the two remaining arms.

Returning to Hole 251-N9 was her next priority. She successfully navigated back to the hole while avoiding too much debris. Without an asteroid and a third arm, the darkship's profile was smaller. Passing through the hole was much easier. Once through, Lyla activated the commlink.

"Catcher 1065, can you read me?"

"Yes, Darkship 3. We read you," Torg's voice answered. "Glad to hear your voice. What's the status of the asteroid?"

"On the way to the sun," Lyla said, feeling relieved. "However, I recovered a disabled escape pod of some sort. I think my missing shipmates are on board, but they're unresponsive. Can you assist?"

"Affirmative. We're on our way," Torg said.

Lyla breathed a sigh of relief.

○ ● ○ ● ○

Jason was standing in the woods filled with trees of brilliant yellow and orange leaves. He grinned at the awesome beauty. As he turned he saw a structure, probably a dwelling. It looked like an old house from Earth, but he had never seen a picture of one exactly like it.

He could see two people on the front porch, an older woman and a child. They were huddled together on a swing, drinking cocoa. *How do I know what cocoa is?* No such beverage existed on Refugia. *How do I know what they're drinking?*

"Time to get changed for bed, young lady," the older woman said.

The little girl obediently hopped off the swing and walked into the dwelling.

Jason saw the woman was Elizabeth Redstone.

"Elizabeth?"

She looked around as if she had heard him but not seen him. Jason walked closer.

"Elizabeth, it's me, Jason."

"Jason?" she said, not sounding as if she recognized him.

"I remember leaving Sector L. Reese and I were escaping in a pod. How am I here with you?"

Jason strained to remember it all: being in the pod with Reese, the space-borne cyborg and Reese shaking him off by rolling the pod. Had he been recaptured by the Logicus?

"Elizabeth?"

Elizabeth's face displayed no recognition of what he was saying.

"Don't you remember me? What about the Logicus?"

Elizabeth again showed no sign of recognition. Then the scene faded. Another face appeared, one he didn't recognize. The face was an older man's face, slightly deformed.

"Dr. Ford?" the man said. "My name is Yurasti. You are safe."

○ ● ○ ● ○

Reese felt a heaviness pressing up against her back. Her eyes slowly opened. She wasn't sure if she was looking up or down. And then a face popped into her view. It wasn't one she would have expected. It was Lyla Covarti.

"Hey, look who's awake," Lyla said.

"Lyla, what are you doing here?" Then Reese realized she didn't really know where "here" was. She lifted her head and looked around. It appeared to be some sort of medical facility.

"How are you feeling?"

"Fine," Reese said. "How did I get here?"

"I found you floating in that pod. I was able to grapple onto it with the darkship I was joyriding in—"

"You were flying a *darkship*? The kind that grabs onto asteroids? Why?"

"Oh, you know about them?" Lyla said. "Well, I was hijacking one. Didn't know there were three others until it was too late. Did a heck of a job on one of their habitats. After I lost my asteroid, I turned back. Then I saw that little pod of yours darting back and forth. I tried to make contact, but I don't think you could hear me. So I used the darkship's grappler arms to scoop you up and bring you to the nearest drydock. And here we are."

"Where's Jason?" Reese asked.

"Next room," Lyla said. "He's kind of out of it."

"I want to see him." Reese sat up in bed.

"Easy there," Lyla said. "You need to rest."

"*I want to see him!*" Reese threw her legs over the side of the bed and stood up. The room started to spin.

Lyla grabbed Reese and stabilized her.

"Maybe this is not really such a good idea," Lyla said.

Undeterred, Reese started walking toward the door. Lyla held onto her to keep her balanced. They came into a circular medical monitoring station of some sort.

"One room over," Lyla said, guiding her to the right.

In the next room, she saw Commander Enberg and Yurasti talking while standing over an unconscious Jason.

"Reese, you're up?" Enberg asked. "How are you feeling?"

"A little wobbly," she said, "but okay."

"Yes, a bit of dehydration and partial asphyxia," Yurasti said. "Those old pods were not designed for long-range travel. I'm glad to see you alive and well. I take it Brother Maynberc wasn't so fortunate."

"No, but he saved us from the decompression," Reese said. "How is Jason doing?"

"Obviously, he's been through a neurological trauma," Yurasti said. "Did he complete the Logicus conversion process?"

"No," Reese said. "We got to him in time."

She took Yurasti's frown as skepticism.

"Maynberc agreed," Reese insisted.

"Well," Yurasti said, "we have neurological tests we can run. In the meantime sleep is an ancient remedy that still works."

"How long since he's been conscious?" Reese asked.

"It's been about seven hours since your pod was recovered. Dr. Ford's drifted in and out of consciousness. During one of his more lucid periods, he asked for you. He also seemed to be interested in someone named Elizabeth."

Reese didn't respond.

"Who is this Elizabeth person?" Yurasti asked.

"Someone he met in Sector L."

"A Logicus?"

"No. I think she was a fellow prisoner," Reese said.

"Lost, I presume."

"I'm not sure," Reese said, annoyed at being interrogated by Yurasti. "I think I'd like to lie down again."

"Are you feeling ill?" Enberg asked.

"No, I just feel tired." She gave a barely perceptible nod of her head.

"Let me walk you back to your room," Enberg said. He held onto her arm to prevent her from falling. Once back in Reese's room, he asked, "You have something to tell me?"

"Commander, in the pod is a case that Jason insisted on bringing back with us. He said it has memories of a person who lived on Earth, someone named Elizabeth."

"Some sort of recording?"

"Jason felt it was something more. He referred to it as a Holy Grail, whatever that is. He thinks of her as a real person. But maybe that's a side effect of the Logicus progress."

"Holy Grail," Enberg said. "Jason used that term back on the ship."

"He delayed our escape to recover it," Reese said.

"If we ask for it," Enberg said, "Yurasti will want to know why."

"I know where the pod is," Lyla said, standing in the doorway. "Drydock 299. That's where I carried it to."

"Think they'll let you back in?" Enberg asked.

"Maybe. I'm on pretty good terms with Captain Torg now."

"Torg?" Enberg asked, surprised. "She was pretty frosty on our way in."

Lyla smiled. "I defrosted her."

"Okay. Go see what you can do," Enberg ordered.

After Lyla left, Enberg helped Reese back to bed. "I'm so glad you two are okay."

"Thanks, boss. By the way," Reese said, smiling, "I saw Earth."

"Earth?"

"Well, an Earth eclipse anyway."

"Really?" he said. "The rest of the crew is going to be so jealous. We need to get a closer look."

"I'm ready to leave the Sphere," Reese said. "How about you?"

"That may be easier said than done," Enberg mumbled.

CHAPTER 26

"Symas Graith," Maklund said, sitting behind her desk, fuming, "you and I have disagreed about many things, but I always believed you wanted to do what is best for the people of the Sphere."

"I do," he said.

"By killing thousands of them?"

"They weren't our people," Graith said. "They were Logicus!"

"Classifying people as less than human allows you to kill them. Right?" Maklund said. "It's just an excuse for genocide?"

"Their emotions and sense of humanity were removed."

"They sound more like victims."

"They were a threat to all of us!" Graith snapped.

"They were human beings! Citizens of the Sphere. If they were such a threat, why didn't you report them to me?"

"Because you would have tried to negotiate with them. Madame President, you always believe the best about people. You try to bring people together. And that's a wonderful quality in a politician, at least during peacetime. Look how you blindly embraced the Refugian crew without any proof they weren't hostile."

"They haven't done a thing to hurt us. But you almost cost some of them their lives."

"The Logicus kidnapped Dr. Ford, not me," Graith said. "You gave them full unfettered access to the Sphere, making it easier."

"So you're blaming me?"

"No," Graith said, shaking his head.

"You are *a mass murderer*."

"But the Logicus are fanatics. They literally remove the emotions from people, *against their will*. It's the most hideous atrocity I can think of. And they intended it for all of us."

"Yes, you already explained that. And I've read the report," Maklund said. "You've put me in a precarious situation."

"I agree," Graith said. "And I'm honestly sorry for that. But at least I've given you deniability."

"Deniability? I can't deny Sector L was destroyed. Thousands of lives lost!"

"You can tell everyone it was a rogue asteroid, one my department failed to catch. I'll take full responsibility. You can call for my resignation. And I'll give it without reservation."

"Resignation? Is that what you're hoping for? You should be put on trial for genocide." Maklund rubbed her eyes. "Then there is the *Sarania* situation."

"Why do you care so much about them?"

"We need them," Maklund said.

"Why?"

"Just like you kept me in the dark, you are in the dark about other things as well. And given your crimes, I'm not inclined to share any information with you."

"Regardless of what you do to me, understand we have identified over 3000 Logicus who are still operating in various habitats."

"Are you negotiating?"

"No, I'll make the list available to the security directorate without any condition. Despite the horror, I am dedicated to the protection of the Sphere."

"But who will protect the Sphere from you?"

○ ● ○ ● ○

Lyla knocked on the entrance to Enberg's office. "I understand Maklund might not open the doors."

"It's a possibility," Enberg said.

"Well, I think I might be able to hack into their systems," Lyla said. "We might be able to open the doors remotely."

"Stop. Just stop," Enberg said. He turned away, then turned back. "I guess it's time for a talk. That was a very reckless thing you did. What do they call it? Riding the rock? Through a hole in the Sphere?"

"Yeah, but I saved Reese and Jason."

"True, and we're all grateful for that. But you had no idea they were in Sector L or in need of help when you clamped yourself onto that asteroid. You could have been killed. And we would have lost our best engineer."

"I know," Lyla said. "I've thought a lot about that. Luckily, the asteroid took the brunt of the crash."

"Luckily?" Enberg said. "Luck is not an operating principle on the *Sarania*. A crew member who's reckless can get themselves or others killed."

"I was trying to save lives, even if they were Spherian lives. And I was only risking my life."

"Lyla, you're one of the smartest people I know. And with this crew, that's saying something. But you have to know you're not immortal, no matter how smart you are. An asteroid doesn't care about your IQ or your credentials. Eventually, the probabilities will catch up with you."

"I know."

"Andy followed your example and could have died."

Lyla felt those words like a stab to the gut, a stab she knew she deserved.

"I know that, too. Commander, I know I'm a risk-taker. I'm arrogant. But I'm beginning to understand my limits."

"I hope that's true," Enberg said.

"What are we going to do about the doors?" Lyla asked.

"I'm having a meeting with Maklund shortly."

○ ● ○ ● ○

Two hours later Enberg and Reese were ushered into Maklund's office.

"Commander Enberg," Maklund said. "I'm glad to see you have mended. No more cane."

"Thank you, Madame President. It was just a minor fracture. Doc Skonauer is a whiz at mending bones."

"And Dr. Monsell, I've read the reports of your ordeal. You're a courageous woman."

"I was just trying to help a member of my crew," Reese said.

"Speaking of which, how is Dr. Ford?"

"He is recovering," Enberg said.

Maklund gestured them toward seats. "I am deeply sorry for what you and your people have endured."

"Thank you," Enberg said, "but that's not why we're here. We've decided to depart the SolarSphere."

"Because of this Logicus business?"

"No, our mission is still exploring Earth. It's what Jason Ford refers to as our Holy Grail," Enberg said. Seeing the confusion on Maklund's face, he quickly added, "I don't quite understand the phrase either. But it's our goal."

"Also," Maklund said, "your Contract requires it."

"That leaves the question of whether you will try to stop us," Enberg said. "I haven't forgotten you asked us to stay and help fortify the genetic diversity of your population."

"It is a matter of our survival," Maklund reminded him.

"We're not unsympathetic. So, we have a compromise. I've spoken to my crew. They have all agreed to donate genetic material, specifically stem cells, sperm and eggs, which you may use in vitro or in vivo."

"In addition," Reese added, "Doc Skonauer and I have analyzed some of your food. I believe your diet may be a contributing factor. Many of your foods are overly processed, becoming quite low in nutritional value, particularly some components of the Unity Dish you served. A change of diet might contribute to alleviating the problem. I would suggest your scientists analyze the relationship of fertility to the nutritional content of the food."

"I wonder why none of our scientists considered this," Maklund said.

"Commander Enberg tells me this is a tightly held secret," Reese said. "I suspect the people working on the problem are geneticists, not nutritionists. Am I right?"

Maklund nodded. "As a nutritionist, you could make a great contribution to our society, perhaps save it. And we would reward you greatly."

"Actually," Reese said, "I'm not a nutritionist either. I'm an environmental biologist. And Commander Enberg has already explained your generous offer. But we have been given a mission by our planet. How could I live with myself if I betrayed that trust?"

Maklund turned to Enberg. "Then your answer is no to our offer?"

"I'm afraid so, but we'll give you the genetic material we offered, as well as Reese's findings. Isn't that enough to get you to open the doors on Drydock 168?"

○ ● ○ ● ○

Jason floated on board the *Sarania*. It felt like returning to a childhood home. *At least there's no Krelax here.* Even though he had only been away for a few days, he did not feel he completely belonged there anymore. It felt like he had spent a year in the Logicus world. Jason was greeted by Kai Herstonick. He was glad there was no larger gathering to welcome him back. After his experience he wanted to avoid crowds.

"Hey, Jason," Kai said. "Good to see you. How are you feeling?"

"Good. Thanks."

"I've cleared your schedule of any duty shifts until you feel up to it."

"Thanks," he said. "Where's the Commander?"

"He and Reese are meeting with President Maklund." Kai looked at the case Jason had in tow. "What do you have there?"

"Just some souvenirs."

"Ah."

After getting settled in his quarters, Jason made his way to Lyla's workshop.

Lyla looked up from her monitor.

"Hey, stranger. How are you feeling?"

"Better," he said.

"What can I do for you?"

"First, I wanted to thank my favorite contrarian again for the rescue."

"My pleasure. To be quite honest, it was the most exciting part of my journey."

Jason chuckled. "Yeah, mine, too. A little too exciting."

"I'm sorry. I didn't mean to—"

"It's okay. I have a request, one I hope isn't too intellectually challenging."

"Oh, now you're just baiting me," Lyla said, giving Jason a disapproving look. "What is it?"

Jason pulled out the bullet-shaped memory core from the case.

"Is that one of the items from the case I recovered from the pod?"

Jason nodded. "Within this device is the living human memory of a human being who lived on Earth. I spoke with her while the Logicus were trying to perform their process on me."

"Living memory," Lyla said. "Are we talking about artificial intelligence?"

"Based on human memories, not machine learning," he said. "She has knowledge that will be invaluable. What do you say? Up for a challenge?"

"*Up for a challenge?* Look at you, trying to appeal to my ego." Lyla just smiled after that.

○ ● ○ ● ○

Several days later after goodbyes and a departure ceremony, the *Sarania* departed Drydock 168. Andy Barosi set a course above the orbital plane and around the upper edge of the incomplete SolarSphere.

Jason floated onto the flight deck.

"How are you feeling?" Enberg asked.

"Better. Ready to resume my duties. But I do have a question. How did you get President Maklund to approve our going to Earth?" Jason asked.

"Technically, she didn't," Enberg said. "Maklund only agreed to open the doors. Once we set a course for Earth, we'll be violating their laws. Maklund will argue to the Spherical Council that opposing us might make an enemy of Refugia. I guess we'll have to trust her political instincts."

"She's a clever woman. I just hope she's clever enough to deal with what's left of the Logicus."

"Me, too," Enberg said. "In the meantime, are you up to taking a bridge duty shift tomorrow morning? Given what you've been through, it's okay if you're not."

"Thank you, Commander. I'll be ready."

After leaving the flight deck, Jason made his way to the mess to locate Reese. He found her a viewport, watching the habitats under construction as the Sarania passed over the upper edge of the incomplete SolarSphere. She turned and smiled at him. Jason reached for her hand and kissed her. Reese smiled back.

"What took you so long?" she asked.

"Sorry," he said, "I just had to clean some old ghosts out of my head."

Reese kissed him back.

Within a few hours Earth was large enough to be seen with the naked eye. Enberg keyed his collar mic.

"Attention all crewmembers. If you're near a window or a monitor, I hope you're looking at that strange little globe ahead of us, Earth. Now our next adventure begins."

ABOUT THE AUTHOR

J.R. Bale has always tried to explore the themes in his stories from an unusual perspective, whether it was politics in *Phoenix in the Middle of the Road* or consciousness in *Cognition Chronicles*. In his pursuit of diverse perspectives, he has traveled to over a dozen countries across four continents. He even applied to NASA's space program. When not writing books, he is a marketing consultant and college professor.

You can learn more about him and his projects at www.jrbale.com.

A NOTE FROM THE AUTHOR

I hope you enjoyed this book. If so, I ask a small favor, not simply for me, but for all authors. If you appreciate a book, any book, please write an online review. The best place for your comment is Amazon, the largest bookseller in the world. Another important site is goodreads.com. It doesn't need to be extravagant. Just let people know you liked the book.

In a world of marketing algorithms, a personal endorsement carries a lot of weight. It's a way of thanking and encouraging authors. It is a random act of kindness, and the world needs more of those.

www.ingramcontent.com/pod-product-compliance
Lightning Source LLC
Chambersburg PA
CBHW020655120726
47906CB00001B/278